Jude Collins was born the youn[...] school in Omagh and Derry. H[...] then University College Dublin where ne obtained his BA and MA in English. He worked as an English teacher in Canada, contributing radio talks and documentaries for the Canadian Broadcasting Corporation. In 1979 he returned to Ireland to take up a post as lecturer in education at the Ulster Polytechnic, now the University of Ulster. He has been a frequent contributor to BBC Radio Ulster, BBC Radio 4 and BBC Radio 5, and writes a regular column for the *Irish News*. In 1990 his radio documentary on education, *Varying Degrees*, won a Sony Award for Outstanding Service to the Community, and in 1993 he received the Distinguished Teaching Award from the University of Ulster. He is married and has four children. *Booing the Bishop* is his first collection of short stories.

For Laurence —

hot that you would

ever Boo the Bishop!

Many thanks,

JC

April '96.

BOOING *the* BISHOP
and
Other Stories

JUDE COLLINS

THE
BLACKSTAFF
PRESS

BELFAST

• A BLACKSTAFF PRESS PAPERBACK ORIGINAL •

Blackstaff Paperback Originals present new writing, previously
unpublished in Britain and Ireland, at an affordable price.

First published in 1995 by
The Blackstaff Press Limited
3 Galway Park, Dundonald, Belfast BT16 0AN, Northern Ireland
with the assistance of
The Arts Council of Northern Ireland

© Jude Collins, 1995
All rights reserved

Typeset by Paragon Typesetters, Queensferry, Clwyd

Printed in England by The Cromwell Press Limited

A CIP catalogue record for this book
is available from the British Library

ISBN 0-85640-567-1

to Maureen, Phoebe,
Patrick, Matt
and Hugh

CONTENTS

THE TRUTH ABOUT BABIES

PRESUMER LIVINGSTONE AND ME, we avoided Frankie Dalton. He was too clean – all shiny hair and trimmed fingernails and *short trousers that had a crease in them*. If he came over when we were playing marbles, we'd pretend the game had just ended and start wrestling with each other. If he held up a shiny brown chestnut on a bootlace, we'd tell him we'd left our conkers at home, although we could feel them in our trouser pockets as we spoke. Once Presumer and me even hid in a school lav, with our feet on the bowl and our backs against the door, for a full half-hour. Frankie had said he'd meet us after school to show us a Desperate Dan story from the *Dandy*, we'd laugh ourselves sick when we saw it. We could hear him moving around the cubicles, calling our names. He even tried to push open our door but we leaned hard against it and kept perfectly still. Eventually he gave up. We didn't hate Frankie; just didn't like being in the same area as him. There was something about him made you want to rub spit in his hair.

But then one October day in fourth class, everything changed. It was during break and Presumer was just getting his breath back after beating his own speed record for drinking milk (a bottle in six seconds) when Frankie put his empty bottle neatly in the crate and announced that his mother was trying to have a baby. Presumer stopped rubbing his stomach and I stopped sucking the bottom of my bottle. Neither of us, you see, was completely clear on babies. Presumer was an only child and I was the youngest in our house, and you heard that many different versions.

Frankie knelt and folded down the tops of his white ankle socks. What you needed to have a baby, he said, was a man and a woman. Presumer nodded, so I did too. The woman's job was to sit in a chair and write a letter to a headquarters place that gave out babies. The man's job was to buy a stamp and take the letter for posting. Lucky enough, Frankie said, his daddy was a postman, so he could deliver the letter for nothing. His mammy felt pretty sure that when Daddy and her put their heads together, the baby would come. Presumer's eyebrows pulled together and he glanced my direction but he didn't say anything. Neither did I.

From then on, any time I saw Mrs Dalton I studied her carefully. She had soft neat features and smiled a lot, and when she saw me staring at her, she smiled even wider. The clean skin and shiny hair that were annoying in Frankie looked nice on her. She wore brighter clothes than the other mothers and she wasn't half as fat. But no matter how long I looked at her I still couldn't make out if she was a woman who had had a baby delivered in the post that morning or a woman who just went in for a good bit of smiling. Like most grown-ups, her conduct made little sense.

In the weeks that followed, Presumer and me began to treat Frankie differently. We still didn't like the way he never got shouted at by the teacher for having dirty ears, nor the way his sandwiches at lunch time always had the crust cut off and were shaped like triangles. But the trying-for-a-baby story had hooked our imaginations. We began to let him hang around us when we were playing marbles or chasies. In between games and sometimes during them we would quiz him for more detail about the letter-writing and how many teeth the baby would have when it came. Frankie would put his hands carefully into the pockets of his pressed trousers and talk about pink writing pads and special deliveries and babies that had twenty-two teeth. You could see he enjoyed being able to give us answers.

And then one April morning Presumer caught my eye across the classroom and gave a thumbs-up sign. 'The letter!' he mouthed, making a rocking motion with his arms. 'Frankie's oul' doll got her parcel!'

They called it Matthew Patrick – or when Mrs Dalton was changing his nappy, which was a lot of the time, 'my wee magpie'. We knew this because Presumer and me used to follow Frankie home. We'd kick a tennis ball around the yard until Frankie came out. Then we'd let him make a couple of feeble kicks at it so we could walk home with him, one on either side. Don't ask me why his mother let us in – a normal woman would have told us to clear off to hell. But Mrs Dalton wasn't normal. She smiled and rattled around in the kitchen and said we were three great chums, Sean, Jimmy and Frankie, which was a lie if ever I heard one. 'Have a word with the wee magpie,' she'd say, starting to peel spuds or polish the mirror over the fireplace. 'He's dying for a chat.'

Obediently we'd tiptoe over to the corner of the room where the baby's pram was. 'Hello!' I would say, but after that I could never think of anything else. Frankie wasn't much better, which was worse, because a person should be able to talk to their own brother. Presumer, though, had no problems talking to the baby. My mother said Presumer could have talked to the Pope.

Presumer's real name was Sean Livingstone, but all he got from most people was Presumer, after the great African explorer. He had greasy hair, buck teeth and when you stood close to him there was a funny stale smell. The days that he came to school, which wasn't every day, he'd arrive late and without a pencil. Sums and spelling words always gave him trouble: he didn't so much get them wrong, as forget he was supposed to be doing them. Punishment didn't make him yell or whimper, the way it did the rest of us. The Brother would be bent forward, hammering at Presumer's hands with the strap, and Presumer would be smiling past him with scummy teeth, his thoughts somehow elsewhere. But there was one thing Presumer was very good at: playing the mouth organ. He was self-taught and terrific. Every year the Brothers' Christmas concert programme would say 'INTERVAL, S. Livingstone, harmonica' and Presumer would stand in front of the curtain and play 'Rudolph the Red-nosed Reindeer' and 'Jingle Bells' and 'Silent Night', and the crowd would whistle and stamp.

So when Frankie's mother said to talk to the baby, Frankie and I would stick our hands in our pockets and make embarrassed faces at each other. But Presumer would lean his face into the pram, a strip of greasy hair dangling from his forehead and whisper: 'Here, wee man – can you fart at all? Close your mouth and push for a Sunday bomb.' And the baby would seem to hear and go red in the face.

'What are you saying to him, Sean?' Frankie's mother would call from the cooker, smiling.

'I'm teaching him to say Matthew Patrick.'

And Mrs Dalton would say 'Aah', or sometimes come over to the pram and say to the baby, with one hand on Presumer's shoulder: 'Come on now, magpie. Tell Sean and Jimmy and Frankie and Mammy a wee wee baby's name!'

The baby never did, but Presumer didn't mind. He just waited until its mother went back to the cooker, then went on encouraging it to do bad things.

When it did – at the first whiff of nastiness – the three of us would shout the news and Mrs Dalton would scoop him up, call him a tricky wee chicken, and take him to the bathroom for changing. As soon as she was out of the room Presumer would collapse on the floor, holding his nose and whispering in a strangled voice, 'Holy Jaysus, I'm gassed!'

And then, when it was six weeks old, the baby died. Since it had been baptised two days after it was born, that end of things was all right – there'd be no question of it ending up in limbo. But at the same time there was no reason for the likes of that to happen, my mother said in a vexed voice. At four on a Sunday afternoon the baby was alive and took a bottle; at seven in the evening it was got dead in its pram. The next day, Monday, Frankie wasn't at school because his baby brother, the late Matthew Patrick, had died and gone to heaven. We all said a prayer for him at the beginning of class. Presumer whispered to me that praying was a load of baloney.

After school my mother reported that Frankie's parents were bearing up well to the shock. Amazingly well, in fact. The house spick and span for people visiting, and both of them shaking hands and chatting. Such control was never seen. In some ways, my mother said, you'd as soon see them roaring and crying – sometimes holding back could affect one inside. Damage them. In fact Mrs Dalton was behaving a bit funny already, God help her. She was refusing to wear black clothes, which was what you were supposed to do if someone died. Wouldn't even hear of a patch of black sewed on her sleeve. And she had sent word with my mother that she wanted me to call that evening to say goodbye to Matthew Patrick. And as if that wasn't enough, she'd sent a second request, which was for me to call and take that half-washed eejit Presumer Livingstone with me. Frankie's mother didn't say Presumer

was a half-washed eejit, my mother said that. She also said that
the blessed woman could go to bits at any minute.

I'd never seen a corpse before, even a small corpse, and the
thought of it wasn't very nice. I tried to tell my mother I had
a pain in my tummy but she said, nonsense, to clean my
face and put on good clothes, it'd soon get better. When I
got there, she went on, I was to be sure to shake hands with
Frankie's mammy and daddy and say sorry for your trouble.
After that you knelt down and said a wee prayer at the side
of the coffin. There was nothing to worry about, anybody could
do it. The baby was in heaven; what was at the house now
was just the remains.

'It'll be like a dead scaldie,' Presumer said, emerging from
his house in a pair of battered white tennis shoes. 'Only
bigger and without the beak.' He stared at my tie and sports
jacket but said nothing. We moved up the hill towards Frankie's
place, Presumer whistling between his teeth and kicking a stone
in front of him.

What happened if the baby started to move in the coffin?
I thought. What if it sat up and made a grab at my hand? What
about all the incidents where dead people came back and said
they were lonely, they'd never rest until they had some company with them in the grave?

'You look as if you're going to throw up,' Presumer
told me, going on tiptoe to flip the knocker of Daltons'
front door.

Mr Dalton, wearing a charcoal grey suit with a waistcoat,
gave a weak smile and gestured for us to come in. His face
looked like a creased shirt.

The living room was crammed with people drinking tea,
smoking, chatting quietly, looking up to see who were the
latest visitors. I couldn't see or hear anybody crying.

'Sorry for your trouble,' I said and shook hands with Mr

Dalton. Mrs Dalton, looking very nice in a red frock with a blue sort of scarf at the neck, emerged from a corner of the room, so I said the same thing to her. Behind me I could hear Presumer.

'Sorry for your baby,' said Presumer to Mr Dalton, and to Mrs Dalton he said, 'Sorry for your baby being dead on you.' The ones sitting nearby sat up straighter and glanced from under their eyebrows at each other.

Mrs Dalton squeezed out a smile that reminded me of stretched elastic and brought us a glass of lemonade each. Two armchairs in the corner of the room were parted, and Presumer, Frankie and me were levered into the space between them. Sitting on the linoleum floor, all we could see were trousers or the seams of women's stockings. To identify somebody you had to tilt your head right back.

Presumer turned to Frankie, who was wearing a black tie and looked, if anything, cleaner than usual. 'Where's it at?' he asked him.

'Where's what?'

'The corpse, for flip's sake – did you think I meant the lav?'

'The remains are in the bedroom,' Frankie said, looking serious in a rehearsed sort of way.

'Why aren't you crying?' I asked him.

'Earlier on I cried buckets. I've come round now.'

Presumer peered past a couple of legs. 'Your ma and da aren't crying either,' he informed Frankie. There was a hint of irritation in his voice. 'It's a big loss, a baby. When you suffer a loss like that, you need to bawl your head off. And then people comfort you until you cheer up.'

'How do you know?'

'My ma told me,' Presumer said, in a voice that gave

Frankie to understand that he, Presumer, would ask any questions that needed asking.

'My ma told me that as well,' I said.

'My auntie told me it years ago, I just forgot,' Frankie muttered, but anybody could see he was lying.

After that, the time went very slow. Your legs get stiff when you're sitting scrunched in between two chairs, and any time we stuck our heads up, somebody seemed to be staring at us. The parish priest came past and patted all three of our heads, and said we were loyal friends to have at a time of trial like this, and Our Lord himself had said suffer little children.

When he went off, Presumer said: 'Anybody would be suffering, stuck in here.' He made mouth-organ-playing motions with his fingers for a few seconds, then turned to Frankie: 'What goes over the water and under the water and never gets wet?' He spoke in a fairly loud voice, and I could feel one or two adult heads peering at us from the chairs on either side.

Frankie frowned, shook his head. 'Under and over ... Tell us.'

'An egg in a duck's backside,' said Presumer.

The three of us went into a fit of giggling that someway didn't match the mood of the room. When we recovered, Presumer tapped Frankie's totally clean knee. 'Here. Are we going to get seeing him?'

'Who?'

'The corpse, your baby's corpse – what do you think? That's what people come for, to see the corpse.'

Frankie didn't reply, just stood up and led the way to the bedroom. As we passed them, people smiled sadly and said, 'The poor wee fellah', to each other. Surprisingly the bedroom was empty of people. The coffin sat at the bottom of the bed, made of brown wood, more like a trunk for clothes really, only smaller and with a pointy end. It rested on two kitchen chairs and was covered in mass cards.

Presumer stared at it, then raised an accusing finger. 'Why didn't you keep the lid open? The lid is supposed to be open until it's taken to the chapel.'

'My mammy wanted it to be like this. She said Matthew Patrick's life had slipped away and it was time to lock the door. So my daddy got a man to close the lid with a screwdriver.'

'Are his eyes closed?'

'I don't know,' said Frankie. 'I wasn't here when they put him in the coffin. Only ones here were my mammy and daddy and later on the photograph man.'

Presumer's hand sank to his side. He stared at me, then back at Frankie. *Photograph man?* Presumer said he'd never heard of a baby being photographed, and he'd double never heard of a dead one being done.

'Well we got my late brother done, so you're wrong. The photograph man used a flash thing. My mammy hadn't a photograph of him, so she got a photograph man to come in and take one. So she'd have it.' He was beginning to sound like our teacher, taking hours to say one thing.

Presumer scratched his oily scalp with one finger. 'But the baby is dead! She'll have a photograph of a dead baby.'

'He looked just like he was sleeping – that's what the photograph man said,' Frankie told us.

Presumer put his eye to the crack where the lid joined the coffin. 'I think I can see him,' he said. 'What's he wearing?'

'A sort of nightdress,' said Frankie.

'What about pyjamas?'

'No pyjamas.'

'A nappy?'

'No nappy.'

Presumer straightened up from the coffin, looking shocked. 'He should have a nappy. Babies are supposed to have nappies – that's how you know they're babies, for flip's sake. If he has no nappy in heaven, God could mistake him for a midget.'

'God doesn't make mistakes,' I said, and as I spoke I felt somebody else in the room. Mrs Dalton was standing in the doorway, very still and pale, not coming in or going out. A couple of times she opened her mouth as if to say something, but no sound came out.

'He does sometimes – doesn't he? Make mistakes.' Presumer, far from being inhibited, was appealing to Mrs Dalton. 'He made the devil – that was a mistake all right. It was in an autograph album I saw once. "God made Satan,/ Satan made sin,/ God dug a big hole/ And threw Satan in."'

Mrs Dalton didn't say anything. I put my hands in my pockets and fidgeted. This was nearly as bad as when she used to ask us to talk to the wee magpie.

'Why has a giraffe a long neck?' Presumer asked Mrs Dalton. And before she could speak: 'To join his neck to his body. What did one wall say to the other?' The shortest of pauses. 'Meet you at the corner.'

And Presumer went straight into a string of riddles, every single one of which I'd heard before. As he spoke, asking and answering them himself, some people appeared behind Mrs Dalton, intent on paying their last respects. But with her back to them she blocked the way, so they stood there, staring past her into the room, looking puzzled. Presumer ignored them, just went on asking riddles, his lazy brown eyes locked on Mrs Dalton's face. Even if she had known what the big chimney said to the wee chimney, he didn't leave her time to answer.

Eventually, after about ten riddles, Presumer paused for breath. By now there were a lot of faces packed behind Mrs Dalton, all of them looking serious and even, I thought, a bit angry. But they didn't exist for Presumer. The only thing in the world was the woman in the doorway, her blue scarf thing in sharp contrast to her red dress. Still watching her, he reached into his trouser pocket and pulled out his mouth organ. I could hardly believe my eyes.

'Will I play "Goodnight, Irene" or "I Discovered a Bum-Bum-Bum" for you?' he asked, resting the mouth organ on his lower lip. Mrs Dalton said nothing, just stood there looking white and swaying slightly. 'Right then, I'll do you the both.'

And he did. He played the 'Bum-Bum-Bum' song first, and his left foot pounded time on the linoleum for the loud bits of the chorus. By this time the entire doorway behind Mrs Dalton was jammed, and Mr Dalton was standing behind his wife, his hand touching her elbow. Still she didn't budge an inch or change her look.

The only thing that had any effect was when, towards the end of 'Bum-Bum-Bum', the parish priest, his face very red, came thrusting through. 'What is the meaning of this?' he boomed in the voice he used for shouting at people who tried to leave the chapel before mass ended. Then Mrs Dalton swung briefly round and said 'Shhhhh!' in such a sharp, piercing way, it was as if not just her mouth but her whole body had gone into producing the sound. The parish priest stopped with his mouth open and said no more. Totally unaffected by the exchange, Presumer geared down to a lower key and the swaying tempo of 'Goodnight, Irene'.

It was a queer feeling, standing there in the room, just Frankie and Presumer and me and the baby's trunk–coffin covered in black-edged mass cards, with all the adults frozen in the doorway like water stuck for a minute at the plug hole. I don't think I ever heard Presumer play as well. His hands moved like butterflies as he vamped the slow-waltz rhythm of the song, head back, eye on the light bulb, body swaying in time. At the door Mrs Dalton swayed slightly too, her face as white as Al Jolson's gloves.

It was only when Presumer had finished and was rubbing the mouth organ on the sleeve of his jacket that Mrs Dalton stopped swaying and began to shake. She could have been a car trying to start, giving bigger and bigger shudders. The people behind her stopped staring at Presumer and turned to her, murmuring and waving their hands more and more as the shudders developed. A couple of them made as if to catch her, but they were all afraid to. It was just as my mother had said: Mrs Dalton could go off in bits like a bomb any minute.

And then she did. The shuddering stopped. A split-second of silence followed. And then her hands with the nails sticking out came up to her face and she let out a long, slow howl that sounded as if she was going to start singing herself, only it was more like a dog being killed than singing, and her nails dug into her own cheeks. The noise rose until it could rise no higher, and then it broke in a sob, a gasping for air, and she doubled up. That's when Mr Dalton's arm went round her shoulders and he half led, half carried her into the other room.

Frankie, his ears red, gave us a watery smile and hurried after her. For a long time, in the distance, you could hear her shrieking. Sometimes there'd be pauses and you'd think it was finished; then it would start again.

It took half an hour for the doctor to come. When he did arrive with his dark blue suit and black bag, he gave her a dose of sleeping tablets that had her conked out before you could say Jack Robinson, my mother said.

As the door closed on her cries the priest led a charge across the room towards Presumer. Up there with him were two or three long faces with big noses that did ushers at the chapel on Sundays. Presumer swung away and his grey gutties squealed on the linoleum as he tried to squeeze under the bed away from them, but it was too late. After a couple of hopeless kicks and punches they had him grabbed, hands and feet pinned tight. His mouth organ clattered free of the ruckus and lay on the floor near the coffin.

'You shameless, sacrilegious guttersnipe you!' the priest yelled. You could see little red veins on the whites of his eyes, and his face had turned the colour of raw meat. 'Have you no respect for living or dead, God or man? Answer me!' His big right hand drew back to strike.

Squirming, Presumer showed his scummy teeth. He wasn't smiling now, he was ripping mad. 'Shut your frigging trap, you holy-poly big pig!' he shouted. 'I was only trying to cheer the bloody woman up!'

As the priest lunged forward to whack the side of Presumer's head, there was a crunching noise – a complete, totally finished, crunching noise. He had stood on Presumer's mouth organ. That's when Presumer began to cry.

Mrs Dalton cried too – for a fortnight without stopping after the baby was buried. My mother said it was a miracle her mind didn't go. But a couple of months later her and her husband were to be seen out shopping together, or walking along the Dublin Road with Frankie on a Sunday. Sometimes going into a shop or crossing a road, she'd reach out and touch Frankie's arm or even his neck. When there was really no need to.

And then ten months later – to the very day, my mother said, and she must have been counting – Mrs Dalton had another baby. They baptised him William Sean, the William after his daddy. Several times Frankie asked us did we want to come up and see it, Presumer and me, but we couldn't be bothered. By this time the two of us were fed up with babies and were more interested in girls, especially ones with chests.

The halloween tree

SHE LIVED IN THE COUNCIL HOUSES a half-mile up the road
from us. When she came down to our farm and aaawed
at the goslings and ooohed at the calves and tried to make the
cat that murdered rats sit on her lap, she seemed like a stupid
girl with eyelashes that needed clipping. My sister Anne was
the one who had brought her to visit in the first place. The
fact that she was three years younger than her gave Anne the
chance to do some more bossing. But even she pulled faces
behind her back. As for me, the way she kept saying she was
a year older than me was beginning to get on my nerves. If
you'd asked me, I'd probably have said she was a puke.

Then Halloween night happened. It was like that song
'Some Enchanted Evening' they played on *Family Favourites*.
I was in the corner of the kitchen trying to crack a walnut
with my heel, only it kept skidding away, when by accident
I glanced across the room. And there she was, coming up
from the white enamel basin with a thrupenny bit between
her teeth. Her hair was plastered to her face, beads of water
clung to her eyelashes, and the teeth that gripped the coin
were small and looked as if they would taste like dolly mix-
tures if you sucked them. The tiled floor tilted beneath my
boots, then shuddered like a wet dog before settling itself.

From that moment I knew that my heart, even my soul that could go to hell if you didn't watch, were hers. Lie, plunder, throw myself off the roof of McCallion's shed – it'd be well worth it, if afterwards she would put her hand under my jumper and stroke my tummy.

'The devil listens to our thoughts if we let him,' the Brother at school had said. How else would you explain the next bit? One minute my sister and her and me were standing outside the front door eating nuts, shouting about whether the apple on the string had been big and nice or just big. Then suddenly Anne had gone racing off down the back field with an empty stout bottle, a skyrocket and a box of matches. I don't remember her saying, 'Let's go down the back field' or 'Where should we go now?' It just happened. And I don't remember why we didn't run after her. But we didn't. Just this girl and me left standing near the drainpipe outside our hall door.

I couldn't stop thinking about her lifting her head out of the water, all wet and shining. Alone with her, my body divided itself into hot and cold bits. Blood rushed up into my cheeks and ears, making them burn. Starved of blood, my oxters started to form icicles of sweat. Desperate, I reached out and steadied myself against the drainpipe. Little bubbles of hard paint had formed on the surface, but they weren't telling me what to do next. Maybe walk across the grass, stare silently into the darkness like Marlon Brando in that film where he got thumped. Then she'd come up behind me and put her arms around my middle, but I still wouldn't look at her. Or would something more direct be better? Throw her to the ground the way John Wayne did in *The Quiet Man*, shower her upturned face with burning kisses?

Suddenly she spoke. 'Would the two of us do a dander out the lane? Be great with that moon, I bet.' Normally she had a bookish way of talking, got from her mother who spent her time reading love stories out of the library, Anne said. Maybe the moon had affected her brain – 'do a dander' – she sounded like my uncle from Donegal. Brother Bozo said that being a lunatic meant you went mad every time the moon came out.

Already she had a five-yard start on me. The boy, was supposed to be in the lead in this kind of thing, wasn't he? Too late for that now. Swallowing a big piece of spittle, I trotted out the lane until I'd caught up with her, then we walked on. The strip of grass growing along the middle divided us like a sword.

Coming home from the pictures alone, I would squeeze my eyes shut when I got to this lane and whisper, 'Sacred Heart of Jesus, I place all my trust in Thee.' Tonight I didn't need the Sacred Heart. Tonight, as if a Hollywood director had taken charge, there was moonlight. Everything – the hedges, the trees, the hardened pats of cow dung on the grass verge – looked as if it had been dipped in whitewash. Even my partner's face was milky blue. With her eyes closed and chin up towards the sky, she looked like one of those Roman pictures with no eyeballs in the history book. How she could walk like that and not hit into something?

I was about to ask her when she opened both eyes and pointed dramatically at the sky. 'Did you ever think about what all things the moon has seen?'

This was a difficult question. I had noticed the map shapes on the moon, like on a geography globe only white. And people sometimes talked about the man in the moon or the moon's face, though I'd never seen either. What did she mean, things the moon had seen?

'That moon has looked down on every thing that ever was,' she said, as if reading my puzzlement. 'From the day of

dot. If a thing happened, the moon saw it. Brian Boru, the
Battle of Waterloo, the Slaughter of the Innocents.' Her
voice dropped. 'What's more, anybody that ever lived looked
up at that same moon. Our Lord's eyes have gazed upon that
moon. Compared to it, we're two skittery wee specks.'

I slowed down, listened to my feet scrunching on the
gravel. This didn't sound quite right. 'What about a kitten
that died before it was two days old with its eyes still not
opened? It would have lived but it wouldn't have looked at
the moon.'

'There's a bit of a difference between a dead kitten and
Our Lord. You're good gas, but.' She leaned across the
middle of the lane and poked me with her elbow as she
said this.

Immediately, for no reason I could see, my mind filled
with an image of her oxter. I tried scrunching harder with
my feet on the gravel. I hated even thinking about oxters.
Sometimes Anne wore a blouse with no sleeves that showed
dark flashes. The oxter which was filling my mind at this
minute had no hair, which at least was something to be
grateful for. But even as I watched, it was blotted out by the
oxter of a Russian shot-putter who had appeared on the back
page of the *Irish News*. Trying not to pant, I pushed towards
the surface again, back into the world of conversation.

'Did you ever hear that song "Blue Moon?"?' she was saying. Afraid my voice might be trembly, I shook my head
silently. 'Doo doo,' she sang, 'Doo-doo-doo doo-doo, doo
dooooo.'

We were nearing the turn in the lane. On the hill in the
distance a car's lights jabbed at the night sky. Without even
bothering to make up an excuse, she crossed over to my side
of the grass strip. For a minute or so she walked beside me,
her shoulder bumping against mine with every second step.

'Do you know the best thing about Halloween?' I tried not to gasp. Hands under jerseys? Oxters? 'Spirits.'

'Spirits?'

'Ghosts. You know. If you're in a coffin, you can't move. So your blood can't circulate and you get pins and needles. And bedsores. Have you ever seen bedsores? Count yourself lucky,' she said, before I could answer. She shook her head and clicked her tongue four times. 'My Auntie Maggie was covered in them.'

'Ghosts don't have blood,' I said softly. I didn't want her to think I was trying to pick a fight, but what she'd said was wrong. 'If you don't have a body, you can't have blood. Ghosts have no body.'

'Who said anything about ghosts?' There was a sudden edge to her voice. 'Corpses – what's inside a coffin before they screw down the lid. The remains. That's what I'm talking about.'

'But you said blood circulating. A corpse has no blood circulating – if it had, the worms would drink it.'

In the moonlight her eyes glittered with contempt. 'There are very few worms in the world' – she tapped my shoulder with her knuckle – 'that drink blood. Very very few indeed.' She dragged her feet through the gravel. 'Anyway, I'm looking forward to being dead. Bet it's like being hugged by somebody really really big.'

As she finished speaking, very close to us across the fence a sucking sound came out of the darkness. It was followed immediately by a heavy sigh. She grabbed my shoulder: 'Sweet Jesus, Mary and Joseph! What is it?'

It was impossible to tell if she was pretending or not. I explained how the cows stood in the mucky part near the feeding trough, then pulled out their feet to move. Suuuck. The effort made them gasp.

'Sounded like a man being sick. You should have warned me. A woman my mammy knows, her hair fell out after a fright like that.'

It sounded as if the girl I loved was blaming me for the cattle standing in the muck. And for not having known she'd be frightened by them. Did she think I was a fortune-teller or something?

At the point where the lane turned at right angles before running down to the road, she sensed that I was a bit annoyed and took my arm. 'Will I tell you a secret? About my mammy?' I nodded. 'She's suffering from night's starvation.' An image of her mother in bed, white and hollow-cheeked, filled my mind. 'Daddy's a dead loss in that department,' my companion said, and spat into the hedge.

By now we were approaching the big tree. It was huge, with a trunk like a rhinoceros's middle. The lower branches draped across the lane, shading it from the moonlight, then dipped their edges into the darkness of the field beyond. On your own, this was the worst part to get past. Head down, coming home from the pictures, I had once heard the rustle of clothing, followed by a stifled laugh. Moaning, I swivelled my gaze, ready to see an angel or a devil come to ask me to build a cathedral or murder someone. Instead, two dark shadows interlacing each other: a courting couple. Too weak to tell them this was our lane, private property, I stumbled past on wobbly legs.

The girl I loved had no such fears. For her the tree was just a tree. Her mother's problems forgotten, she was striding into its shadow, drawing me after her by an invisible thread. One small white hand reached up and patted the trunk, as if it was a horse's bum. 'It says in a book at home that the Irish used to worship trees. And if you cut down a tree, they would have your body cut in the same place.'

'What if you cut off a branch?'

'They'd take an arm. Two branches, two arms; three branches, threee . . . three branches, two arms and a leg. And so on.' She pointed to where the bark of the tree had been cut away. 'Now that's nice.' Maybe half a dozen pairs of initials had been carved into the tree, some so clumsily you couldn't tell what they said. She put a finger in the grooves of each and ran it round slowly. 'Beautiful, really. Imagine taking a knife to a tree, to testify to your love. This one even has a heart round the initials.'

Was she hinting that I should take out my penknife? 'Kills a tree, that,' I told her. 'Daddy says if he got ones cutting his good tree he'd brain them.' It was time to change the subject. I pointed to the base of the tree. 'Bet you never saw those before. Poison toadstools.'

She shook her head. 'I'm familiar with toadstools and those are mushrooms.'

I laughed softly. 'Try eating them, then. Boy at our school swallowed two wee ones and they were hours pumping out his stomach.'

She peered more closely. 'Oh, you're right. They are toadstools – didn't notice the brown edge. I bet there was ones came here with a death pack,' she said, nudging the base of the tree with her toe. 'Tears in their eyes and sorrow in their hearts. Ready to carve their initials before walking into Death's dark kingdom.'

'Its what?'

'Dark kingdom. Because their love can never be. They make this pack, you see – it's a, a sort of parcel where you put stuff that kills you. And you leave a wee note stuck to a tree with a dagger saying, "We could not live without love."' She leaned against the tree, stretched her arms above her head like a ballet dancer. 'Have you ever imagined killing yourself? Or somebody killing you?'

I shook my head and tried to look convincing. I was remembering the spiders I used to catch in a jampot. A square of cardboard over the top, trotting to the cooker, where I would tip them onto the hotplate. Briefly they'd dance along the surface until their little legs shrivelled. Legs gone, the dot body stopped and turned into a tiny black flake.

'Hens,' I said. 'I've killed millions of hens.'

'Have you? What with?' Her eyes were glittering again.

'You take the feet in your left hand, up in the air' – I demonstrated – 'and the neck between your fingers with your right hand, and you twist and you pull. At the same time.' I mimed the action. 'The trouble is, you can run out of pulling room.' It was the truth. More than once I had been faced with a hen that was longer from neck to toe-tip than I could stretch. A half-strangled hen jumps and flap its wings so hard it pulls you in a zigzag all over the yard. 'If you ask me, a hatchet is kinder.'

Her hand went to her mouth. 'You're a desperate man – a hatchet!' Her fingers slipped down her throat onto her chest.

When I saw her doing that I felt as if something was squeezing my stomach from the inside, just behind my bellybutton. To distract myself I leaned and plucked a toadstool, held it close to my mouth. 'Would you like to see me take a bite?' Her eyes grew even rounder, the light glistening on the white bits. 'I will if you want. To show you that I . . . Just to show you.'

She guessed what I had been about to say. Must have. With one movement she plucked the toadstool from my hand, flipped it over her shoulder and placed her other hand at the back of my neck. I'd had a haircut two days earlier and her fingers felt tickly. 'You're a right wee rascal, Jimmy Rice,' she said, moving her hand up to tug gently on longer bits of hair. 'C'mere this instant.'

Her arms, it suddenly struck me, were very long. Perfect for pulling hen's necks. Maybe that was her plan for me. Trick me into going for a walk, talk rubbish, then queeekk. I smiled and moved back a step, letting my arms hang loose but staying on the balls of my feet.

Whether that put her off or not, I don't know, but next thing she'd taken her hands away and walked to the tree trunk, which she leaned against. Smiling, she patted the space beside her. 'C'mere, you scamp. I want to chat.'

Cautiously, I joined her.

For the next ten minutes, with our shoulders touching, she talked in a low steady voice about A Certain Girl. She wouldn't give names, there was no good me asking her, she said, because that'd be name-dropping, and people who dropped names made her feel sick. But this girl had long brown hair and glasses and lived in John Street and was the worst sickener my companion had ever met. She may have said why she was such a sickener, but I don't remember. I kept noticing how bright were the eyes of the girl I loved, how her voice went up and down when she became annoyed, how a strand of hair kept dripping forward from behind her ear to dangle in front of her face until she flicked it back, where it immediately began to inch forward again. And there was the matter of being able to feel the warmth of her shoulder touching mine, right through the material in her coat and the material in mine, as we stood side by side, our backs against the tree trunk.

'And if it is chickenpox she'll be disfigured for life.' She nodded in agreement with herself, then straightened up and peered into the darkness on either side. 'I wonder, could I go somewhere.' She pointed. 'Hold you the barbed wire down a minute until I hop over. Won't be a tick.'

The night-time seemed bigger without her. Sounds came from the darkness, which made my face burn. Down in the distance of the Drumquin Road, a dog barked.

'Listen.' Her voice was a nervous whisper, almost a whimper. 'Is there cows in this bit? I can hear something.'

This was tricky. If I said yes, she might panic and come tumbling back over the fence, knickers round her knees. If I said no, there were no cows in that field, she might think it was ghosts and pass out. Then I'd have to go over the fence and, oh my God, pull up her knickers, and carry her unconscious body some way back over the barbed wire.

'There are a couple of cows,' I shouted, 'but they're really wee. And tame.' It was a lie but I had to say it.

'Phhhew.' Silence for a moment, then a strong hiss that kept going for longer than I would have thought possible. Part of me felt a bit sick, another part warm and glad. To think a girl could be so relaxed in my company she was prepared to do a number one! True enough, I couldn't see her and she didn't realise I was listening, but it still showed I had impressed her. The minute she came back I would kiss her.

But once more she was ahead of me. As she hopped down from the wire onto the grass bank beside me she stumbled. I stuck my hand out to help. Immediately her hand was behind my neck, this time gripping my hair. 'You are,' she said slowly, like somebody hypnotised, 'a perfect gentleman.' Then she closed her eyes, pushed her nose against my face and kissed me.

I'd never been kissed on the mouth before. The nearest I'd got was my Auntie Cassie, whose clothes smelled of moth-balls and whose face was stiff with whiskers. Cool and smooth, my companion's face belonged to a different species completely. After the second kiss, she put her cheek against mine. I could smell peppermint, I think, as she gripped my hair harder. 'Oh my love,' she said. It was the way a person would speak if somebody had twisted their arm. Groaning, really.

Unsure what to say, I put my hands round behind her and patted her. 'There, there,' I said, making circular motions on her back. 'You're safe now.'

It made her worse. 'Oh my own honey, Jim,' she said in a slightly American accent, and pulled my hair with two hands.

In the pictures, when the girl and the man put their faces together, the girl's face went sideways and there was nice music. The real thing felt . . . heavier. For a start, her lips were quite thin. And dry and a bit hard as well. How that could be, since they were made of flesh the same as everybody else's, I wasn't sure. Maybe it was the way she had her teeth clenched behind them, or the way she kept pushing against my mouth with them.

In the end I found it so hard to breathe, I pretended to have a cramp in my leg. I bent down and rubbed it, my mind throbbing. So this was the sin of impurity. It wasn't as thundering an experience as I'd imagined it would be. No roaring oceans, like the woman had got in the magazine story in the dentist's. No floating on air. Not even a lot of pleasure, to tell the truth. I straightened and we stood side by side, staring into the darkness. From the far side of the house faint shouts came drifting. 'Will we go back?' I said at last.

We walked on the same side of the lane this time. Or rather she walked on my side. My fists were firmly in my pockets and after the turn in the lane she linked her arm inside mine. I thought maybe she would tell me about other people she had kissed or what she thought of my lips. But she didn't. Instead she talked about a slow bicycle race she'd nearly won at Drumquin Sports the previous summer, only the judge had been the uncle of the girl behind her and had disqualified her even though she'd never once put her foot on the ground. 'Corruption,' she said, and repeated the word twice. 'People like that should be let nowhere near a slow bicycle race.'

Thirty yards from home she suddenly pulled her arm clear. 'Readysteadygo!' she shouted, and was ten yards ahead before I could move. I sprinted for a couple of steps, then slowed again. She had a lead of at least fifteen yards. Why chase what you can't catch? Above the house a rocket went hissing into the night sky, gushing a plume of white and orange sparks.

And for no reason I began to think about the time I had jumped the sheugh at the back of the byre when I was only eight. For a half-hour I had stood beside it, bending my knees and pulling fierce faces at it, but not jumping. With dusk coming down and tea time getting near, I had finally taken a couple of steps back, bit my lower lip and made a staggering leap. By clinging to the grass of the far bank with both hands I'd managed to pull myself up. Only one wellington toecap was smeared in a greasy mess that smelt. I'd done it.

Arms swinging, staring ahead at the sky that had sunk into darkness again, I marched hup, two, three, four towards the house. The next girl I let take me for a walk, I promised myself, would have damper lips and be a slower runner.

Eating and fighting

THE TRUTH IS, I'VE NEVER LIKED ANNE MUCH. I do see more of her over the last eighteen months, since Mickey died. She was in town on a Saturday choosing a hall wallpaper and he was at home watching the television. So the last thing he saw was probably horse-racing. She came into the living room with four different samples and got him lying dead on the floor. Underneath him lay the *Radio Times*. For a while Anne was on nerve pills, got headaches, cried every time somebody even said Mickey's name. But she came round. Women do. Now she's out at painting classes and the Vincent de Paul Society and there's even talk about learning Japanese. I don't think she misses him at all, except when something goes wrong – the boiler stops working or a door handle won't turn. Then she rings me. If I can fix it, I do; if I can't, I arrange for somebody to come and look at it.

She prefers when it's me does the work, I think. Clucks about saying thanks and do I need a wrench and only for me she'd be lost. Afterwards we go into the living room and I sit in the chair Mickey fell out of when he died, and she brings in tea and wheaten biscuits half-coated with chocolate, and three or four KitKats in their red wrappers. The tea is always too weak. We sit and chat about the new curate and whether she needs her glasses changed and how polite the wee girl working in the dry-cleaner's is. You couldn't get a civiler chat. And yet, when I sneak a look at her face, as she stares out the picture window or nibbles like a mouse on the corner of a biscuit, I feel a twitch of dislike for her. Unfair, because in some ways she was every bit as much a victim as me, all those years ago. When I'm feeling a bit out of sorts or tired, I blame our mother. Into myself, that is, not out loud to Anne. If our mother had been there that day, there'd have been no trouble.

Normally she was there on Pancake Tuesday, standing at the kitchen table, everything ready for us. We'd have raced each other the length of our lane – Anne is four years older than me, so she always won. Panting, we'd toss our bags into the space between the chest of drawers and the wall, then flop into our place at the table.

Our mother didn't make pancakes the perfect flat shape you get in shops nowadays. They'd bulge more at one side than the other, and their edges would taper into a crisp brown wafer, sometimes even a black lacy edge. But unloaded on our plates, crusted with sugar and limp with butter, they seemed perfect. Immediately we would start forking them into our mouths, sucking air to cool them as we gobbled. At the cooker our mother went on pouring and scooping, smearing with butter and coating in sugar. For fifteen minutes she kept ferrying fresh helpings, until our mouths hung open and we had difficulty breathing.

The best part was, all this gorging happened the day before Lent. And Lent for us meant sacrifice. Sugarless tea that tasted like paraffin. Slices of bread without jam that scratched the roof of your mouth. No sweets. Visits to the Blessed Sacrament, so boring you felt like whimpering. And a mortification I didn't let on about: in the toilet, for forty days and nights, I sat with the seat up, not down. Pain and deprivation at every turn, deliberately inflicted, to make the soul behave itself. So when we tumbled into bed on Pancake Tuesday, we were literally swollen with righteousness. Tonight had been the feast, tomorrow would be the famine.

But that was before this particular Pancake Tuesday. I was ten and Anne was fourteen, and when we came panting in the door, instead of being at the cooker where she should have been, our mother was in the hall with her coat and hat on. She was slipping down the road, she said, to see Mrs Davey. Wouldn't be two ticks. Mrs Davey was sick with something that kept making her thinner, and word had come earlier in the day that she'd taken a wee turn for the worse.

'She might be in need of her floor swept, or them two wee boys their dinner,' our mother said, picking up her handbag.

We didn't like the Davey boys, who were only in third class and whose noses ran.

'What about our pancakes?' I asked, my voice hoarse with self-pity.

Our mother looked in the hall mirror and touched a wisp of hair into place at the back of her head. It was all right, she said, the mix was made. If she wasn't back by half-four, Anne could pour it carefully from the bowl into the frying pan and put the pan on the cooker. The instructions were written on the lid of a shoe box. But our dinners were in the oven, we must eat them first.

It was quiet and gloomy in the kitchen on our own. Anne sat at the top of the table, reading a woman's magazine. From time to time she'd glance at her plate and spear a bit of stew. Duck her head to bring her mouth nearer the fork. Then she'd go on reading, cheeks bulging and lips barely closed as she chewed. The pendulum clock that my father oiled every first Sunday of the month, using a feather and a bottle of paraffin, made its slow tick that was more a cluck. Outside the window, drops of rain had started to darken the orange roof of the hay shed.

I used the back of my fork to mash my potato, then patted it flat and eased it sideways to mop up an estuary of gravy. I'd manage the sweets all right – everybody would be off them, at least for the first week. And chewing my food thirty times every mouthful was just a matter of counting. You could manage having no hot-water bottle if you rubbed your feet together under the bedclothes. All that stuff would be simple. No, the hard part about Lent was going to be not watching Anne dress herself.

The thing was, I slept in an inner bedroom – to get to it you had to go through Anne's bedroom. My room was small and had a picture of Our Lady with her eyes cast down so she looked half-asleep and a withered blessed palm stuck in the corner of its frame. It was a nice room – below it was the back yard, and beyond that the front field and the rabbit holes along by the hedge leading down to the river. Some mornings, when I had nothing to do, I'd lean my elbows on the window and stare out until my eyes felt glazed. Other times I groped under the bed and got one of the comics stored there, or an Enid Blyton book. But the thing I liked doing best was lying back in bed on a Saturday morning, looking through the half-open door and watching while Anne took off her nightdress and one by one put on her clothes.

Her legs were easily the best part. Especially when she had adjusted her navy blue knickers and pulled her black stockings into place. The part of her legs between garters and knickers oozed out over the tops of the stockings, and how anything could be so round and white and plump was beyond belief. The fact that they were on show for such a short time in a way made it better – no matter how much

I told myself to be ready now, my eyes would barely have adjusted to the sight when the vision would be gone. She'd have wriggled into her skirt, joined some sort of hook things at the side and smoothed the front and back with the flat of her hands before I had time to swallow.

My eyes, if she ever glanced towards me, would be shut. Or at least that's how they would seem to her. In fact I could see perfectly through the bars of my lashes. If she called into me, which she sometimes did, I'd groan faintly, like a man buried under a mountain of sleep. When her dressing was complete and she was bending down to tighten her shoes, an emptiness would fill my heart. It was like when the hobby horses stopped at Bundoran and you had to get off – a brief whirl of music and colour, then life fell back into its drab black-and-white state again. Except that the hobby horses were once a year, during the summer, and Anne's legs were once a week, all year round. That was a consoling thought.

Only now, in a fit of heroism, I'd gone and given the legs up for Lent. Not because they were wrong, but simply because they were enjoyable, like sugar in your tea. I'd have to listen for the sound of the bed creaking as she got out of it. The minute I heard that sound, I would reach under my bed and grab a book or comic, which I'd hold up between her and me. No matter what rustling I heard, and until her footsteps sounded going downstairs, I would keep my eyes on the page. The thing was, would I have the willpower? The Famous Five and Korky the Kat could be exciting to read about, but they didn't hold a candle to Anne's two goose-bumped legs.

Now, in the kitchen on Pancake Tuesday, I put my knife and fork together in the middle of my empty plate and wondered if God would consider an altered package. Say, an extra rosary every Saturday instead, or sleeping without a pillow? The possibilities of a new Lent deal that would leave Anne's legs alone was beginning to form in my mind. But before it had time to develop, the owner of the legs wiped her mouth with her hand, said cabbage should be fed to pigs not humans, and began to make the pancakes.

As she cooked she talked to me over her shoulder, and her mood seemed to improve. She spoke of school, and of a girl called Fidelma Taggart, who smelt. When the nun wanted to punish a girl, she'd put her sitting beside Fidelma. She spoke of a mechanic who worked in Charlton's garage and who stared at her from underneath cars as she walked home. 'His eyes devour me,' she said. She spoke of countries she had studied in geography where they strangled baby girls, and other countries where men had up to fifty wives. 'Once a month the man gets all his wives together in one room. For social purposes.'

And then she began to tell me about Pancake Tuesday in America. The people there didn't call it Pancake Tuesday at all, they called it Mardy Grass. That was because the weather in America is so hot, people go out and sit on the grass every chance they get, and Mardy is the American word for Tuesday. And on the Mardy Grass day they didn't eat pancakes – in the hot American weather, they'd burn the mouth off you. Instead they ate big juicy pears and oranges and bananas that were brought round in baskets by lovely-looking girls, and big black men with really white teeth would stand on chairs and play trumpets. They did too, it was in the bloody magazine. And the girls – you should see the girls, she said with a little smile. The Mardy Grass girls had nothing on them but wee short skirts up to here – the edge of her hand pressed against her thigh – and they served cream meringues and they kissed the men on the mouth, so bits of cream stuck to their moustaches, especially the Negro men, who had curly black moustaches and laughed with their mouths open when they were kissed.

The eating and drinking and music and kissing went on all Pancake Tuesday day and all Pancake Tuesday night. Non-stop. I asked how they managed going to the lav.

'This magazine is written in England,' she said, tapping it irritably. 'They're not going to start talking about going to the lav.' Some of the men, she went on, fell asleep and woke up with sunstroke, and had to have bags of ice held to their forehead for at least six hours by one of the girls. And then at sundown – just about now, she said, waving her hand towards the steady drizzle that had developed outside our window – with the mosquitoes making their melodious call, all the people would get up from the grass and form four lines. Each person would put their hands on the waist of the person in front, and the four big lines would twist and sing their way to the town hall of New Orleans, kicking their legs out sideways in time to the beat. And there the girl with the shortest skirt and the shiniest hair would be crowned Mardy Grass queen, and she'd sit for five minutes on the knee of every man there, and sometimes a black man would get so excited he'd play his trumpet until he burst a blood vessel in his neck and fell off the chair and had to be taken to hospital.

While she told me all this Anne kept poking at the pan with a fork, leaning forward occasionally with her eyes closed to sniff. She looked as if she knew what she was doing, but in fact she was making a muck of things. Maybe she hadn't the pan properly greased, or she cooked the pancakes for too long. Whatever it was, the mixture she brought to the table looked like blackish scrambled eggs.

'It's clustered now, but wait till you see when it settles,' she said, shaking a lump onto my plate.

It lay there in a heap, glistening. When I prodded it with

a fork, a little bit slid down the heap. That must be what she meant by settling. The portion on her own plate, I noticed, was smaller than mine.

'Mmm!' she said, nibbling on a tiny mouthful.

I loaded my fork as heavy as I could and swallowed. The black and brown mess slid down, but left an ashy taste on the roof of my mouth. After two glasses of water from the scullery tap the taste was still there.

'Mmmh,' said Anne, licking her fingers and looking with half-closed eyes at the ceiling. 'Not quite perfect yet.'

With the last batch, she decided our mistake so far had been that we (she kept saying 'we', although she hadn't allowed me near the cooker), we hadn't flipped the pancakes into the air enough, the way Lord Snooty and Keyhole Kate did in the comics. It was the air passing under the pancakes, she explained, that made them nice and fluffy.

Standing with the heavy pan between her bent knees, she swung it violently up to head height and pulled it quickly back down again. Hard work: you had to watch you didn't spill and the pan weighed a ton. After three tries she was gasping, but the mixture was still in the pan. It clung there, like a parachute in a field of treacle. Then suddenly on the fifth go, which she swore was going to be the last, the pancake gave a flop, left the pan and landed on the hotplate of the cooker. Or at least half of it did – the other half, showing a jagged tear, stayed put in the pan. Immediately the air was thick with smoke and hissing.

'Holy hanging Jesus!' Anne yelled, dropping the pan and blowing at the smoky mess on the hotplate. Useless. From what we could see through the smoke, what had been brown and black had turned completely black. Face red, eyes darting, she shouted for me to lift the bloody pan off the floor, did I want the house burnt to a cinder? I tried to lift it, but the handle was roasting and I let it fall to the floor again, splashing what was left in it over the kitchen tiles and our legs. It felt like being stung by a nettle.

I'll have to tell this next bit carefully, because it's hard to explain. I was bending down to retrieve the pan when for no reason everything became blurred. It was like being coshed from behind by a burglar in one of the Bulldog Drummond books. Only of course there was no burglar and I wasn't in a book. What had really happened was, my eyes had filled with tears. No warning. One minute, no thought of crying. Next minute, both eyes brimming. I suppose a lot of things caused those tears – the hot pan handle, the smoke, the taste of burnt pancake in my mouth. But the main reason for my tears and the snot that had now begun to stuff my nose up was the feeling that I was a prisoner. A prisoner of this gloomy kitchen, a prisoner of the rain outside, a prisoner of my promise about Anne's legs.

Why did there have to be a Lent, full of stations of the Cross and statues muffled in purple? How could my sister be so good at bossing and so bad at cooking pancakes? And why above all had God decided that my life was to be lived in this draughty, shadowy country instead of in America, where I could have danced in the sunshine, my hands on the waist of the person in front? I thought again of those black men from the Mardy Grass blowing their trumpets and cradling girls on their knees, none of them knowing or caring that I existed, and the resentment exploded.

'You're a big bossy hairy Mary!' I screamed, straightening up. The snots were tickling my upper lip and through my tears Anne had spears of light coming out from all over her. 'Talk, talk talk – think you were a bloody parrot. Only, a parrot would cook better pancakes than this, this cat's pish!' And I kicked the pan across the floor, where it collided with the bottom of the dresser. Then I pulled my sleeve across my upper lip and faced her, hands on hips.

There was a moment of silence after the echo of the pan had died away. Then with one of her eyebrows higher than the other, she stared from the mess on the cooker, to the pan in the corner, to me. Both her eyebrows came level again then and pulled together, separated only by a V of annoyance. Then she came after me, her nails in the scrabbing position and her clenched teeth showing.

It took her a good while to catch me. As she stalked me she used the time to tell me some things she'd been meaning to say to me, she said, for ages now, only she hadn't thought I was worth wasting her breath on. She still thought that, in a way, but she'd tell me in any case. I was, she explained, a snottery, two-faced wee shite. Smiling and sucking up to people, showing them my first communion photograph with my hair slicked down, butter wouldn't melt, would it? Ha, that was a laugh. For what was I underneath? A whitened speckled cur. A treacherous whining wee white speckled cur that'd try to bite people when their backs were turned. For two pins, she said, when our mother got home, she'd tell her The Truth about me.

'Tell her what?' I asked, my voice wobbling. 'I did nothing.'

When I said that, Anne stopped chasing, raised both hands in the air and gave a yelp of a laugh. 'Listen to it!' she said, as if appealing to an invisible audience. 'Would you just listen to the dirty wee, filthy wee hypocrite!' Then she lunged at me across the table. Was it nothing, she said, that a girl couldn't pull on a pair of stockings but a slimy wee Peep-Tom was squinting at her through a door? That was nothing, was it? Her own brother! She'd thought of turning her back as she got dressed, only that would have made me worse. WOULDN'T IT?

The third time round the kitchen table she managed to hook a finger on to the neck of my pullover, but when I kept on running it stretched and began to tear and she had to let go. One sure thing, she shouted after me, from now on that bedroom door would be shut. I could groan till I took a fit, but I'd get no more open door. She'd get a bar put on it, too, to be on the safe side. If anybody asked, she'd tell them. 'My brother's not right in the head,' she'd say. Other girls' brothers respected them, minded their business, kept their eyes to themselves. But not Mr Peep-Tom. Not Mr Sex Maniac. Gleeking round corners like a lighthouse, morning to night, morning to night. Mad to see if he could see something he hadn't seen before. Well, for my information, when a girl reached fourteen, she had a right to some privacy, some respect. Then she got a grip of my hair and pulled me to the ground. Her breath came in hot pants on my face and her nostrils looked a lot bigger than usual.

And that's where our mother found us – on the kitchen floor – when she came back at ten past five. Anne had her knee in my stomach and a fistful of my hair in her right hand; I had her wee finger bent back as far as I could and we were both moaning and near tears. When we heard our mother open the front door, we tried to scramble to our feet, but she was already reaching for the rod that my father kept propped behind the picture of the Sacred Heart.

She didn't actually use it, just waved it about for a while and shouted. But there was no question of pancakes that night. Anne sidled over and put on her woman-to-woman voice and said it had all been my fault, she'd been trying to *restrain* me, but our mother wouldn't listen. Our mother said she'd always known we were bad articles, but she'd never imagined anything like this. Jumping on each other like roaring lions the minute she stepped out of the house! And, if anything, Anne was worse than me, for she was a big lump of fourteen that should have known better. *And* she was a girl. When *she* was a girl, our mother said for probably the fifteenth time, she used to creep about the house like a mouse, and didn't know the meaning of the word 'bold'. Then we got a slice of bread and raspberry jam each, and a mug of tea, and were sent straight up to bed.

Anne had meant what she said to me. That night, and on Ash Wednesday morning, and every morning after that, her bedroom door was closed tight. It took her a while to get it to close, as the door hadn't been shut in ages and was slightly bent. Now, from where I lay in bed, I couldn't see a thing. Except for the smallest chink where the door had warped. If I stood on the iron rail at the bottom of my bed with my face against the wood, my nose squashed against the hinge, I could still see her. Only then, the cold morning air began to make me sneeze and I had to dive under the covers and hold a fistful of sheet against my mouth to smother the sound.

Two weeks later Mrs Davey died, and the following Pancake Tuesday – a year later – my mother had the pancakes going on the cooker as usual. Only instead of running, Anne walked in the lane after school with an amused look on her face. And when our mother waved a plateful from the cooker, she sniffed and said no thanks, she *knew* what pancakes did to a girl's complexion. No, she explained, what she wanted, if that was all right, was to go to the pictures with Maeve Mulryan – a last visit before Lent? Astonishingly, without even an argument, she was told she could. An hour later, our mother pulled on her old coat and went to the henhouse to collect eggs. Anne, meanwhile, went out the lane smiling with two-and-six in her fist.

Swollen clouds were gathering above the hay shed. Alone, I chewed my way through the two platefuls of pancakes. Each pancake was a further layer of depression on my heart. Anne had escaped, I was still here. Maybe in fifty years' time I'd still be here in this room, with its shadowy corners and slow-ticking clock and nothing to look at only rain on a roof. How much nicer if after He made me, God had dropped me down in America, to let me live my life in the sunny, short-skirted world of the Mardy Grass.

Last week I said something and after I'd said it I wished I hadn't. The cistern in Anne's toilet hadn't been working. So she phoned me and it only took me quarter of an hour to fix it. When I called her in to see it flush, you'd think I'd given her a thousand pounds.

'Thanks be to God,' she kept repeating. She'd had nightmares, she said, about the toilet backing up and the whole place a mess, all the rooms. Then she'd wake up and be afraid to go to sleep in case it really happened.

She'd put the loaded tray down on the stool and was stirring the teapot to get it a bit stronger when I asked if she remembered the day we burnt the pancakes. She stopped with the teaspoon in midair. Pancakes? When we were small, I said. When Mrs Davey was sick and we made them ourselves. Anne puckered her lips, narrowed her eyes behind the glasses, then went on stirring. No, she said, pancakes was one thing she'd never been able to make. Even when she was small. She paused, took a hanky with an embroidered edge from her apron pocket and blew her nose. And these days, with poor Mickey gone, she tried not to think about the past. Too morbid. 'Today, not yesterday,' she said to me, holding over a plate of KitKats. 'Have another one of these.'

So I did.

ONE OF THE BOYS

CAMMY GRANT WAS THREE FEET TALL, had a hump and never played by the rules. When we put people in jail in the school yard, they were supposed to give up their toffee-apple stick and stay in jail. But Cammy, using his squat little legs and his hump for leverage, always squirmed free. 'You have to be touched first!' we'd yell after him. He'd never listen. Down the school yard he'd scurry, smacking his own rear in a sideways run, pausing only to shout bad language at us over his deformed shoulder.

Maybe it was his upbringing had him that way. He lived with his mother in the Back Lane, where you could put a brush handle through the window of the house opposite if you leaned out far enough. In fact Cammy claimed he had, showering broken glass on the bed of a girl with long black hair, who had jumped up with nothing on and stood at the window shouting at him. Later, Cammy said, he'd gone over and had a bath with her. On May afternoons the rest of us would go home with loaded schoolbags to groan our way through exercises for the eleven-plus. Not Cammy. His mother, who wore a turban and smoked, would have gone out, leaving the front door locked and an upstairs window open. Cammy would stand in the middle of the Back Lane, whirl his schoolbag twice above his head and send it arcing neatly through the open window. That done, he was free to spend the evening in the Market Yard, where the men smoked and played pitch-and-toss. Cammy said he wouldn't do an eleven-plus if you paid him.

So this Monday in May we had just come back in from the eleven o'clock milk break. Our teacher was still out in the porch, smoking and talking with the fifth class teacher. We could see their heads like shadows through the frosted glass. From time to time the shadows would move and we'd hear them laughing, the laughter sometimes ending in a cough. Finally at quarter past eleven, five minutes later than usual, our teacher bustled back in and attacked the board with a duster. The chalk dust swirled and dived in the sunlight. On the board he wrote 'P-R-O-V-E-R-B'.

'Right, boys. What's this?'

Caruso Kelly always started things. 'Sir, a kind of boat. A proverb.'

'Sir, sir!' Anthony Dobbins called from the corner of the class, going up and down like a cork in his seat. 'Sir, it's a wee thing in a car engine that –'

'Sir, a proverb is a word.' Big Trigger Donnelly was never wrong but never right either.

Our teacher's face got redder the more answers we gave. 'Shut up!' he shouted at last. 'Shut. Your. Stupid. Mouths.' Turning to the board he wrote, 'A Healthy Mind in a Healthy Body.' 'That,' he said, tapping the board with a nicotined finger, 'is a proverb. It means there's no good being smart if you're sick, and no good being Charles Atlas if you've sawdust in your head. Which is why the fifth class teacher and myself have put our heads together.' He turned to the board and wrote 'B-A-S-K-E-T-B-A-L-L'. 'Now you'll not know this, but the boys that invented basketball were the Red Indians. Played it on all the big occasions. The day Christopher Columbus arrived in America, the beach was full of them, playing away. And when the white men joined in, Columbus's sailors and so on, they were hopeless, compared to the Red Indians. Only a while later the darkies came to America, boatloads and boatloads of them. Some of them eight and nine feet tall. Half as big as me again, three times the size of Grant here. Huge big lumps. So the Red Indians allowed them a game, and it was the worst mistake they ever made. The darkies beat them good-looking.'

There was a silence as we imagined the crowded beach, the giant black figures out-jumping the brown figures.

'Sir, is basketball like handball?' Wanger Duncan asked. 'Just a wee bit like it?'

'If you'd thought for days, Duncan, you couldn't have hit on a game less like. Handball!' As he said the last three words, he leaned over, gripped Wanger's hair and shook his head from side to side. 'No, and it's not a game that's played with bats nor fists nor heading the ball either. Hands down.' He lowered his voice and banged his fist into his palm. Then pointed a finger, moved it around the class. 'Skill. That's what basketball's about. And strength. But above the both of those, do you know what basketball's about? Teamwork.' He stood eyeing us, his lower lip stuck out in a challenge. 'If you're a blurt that's greedy, don't like to pass the ball, then my advice is, stay away from basketball. THE GAME IS NOT FOR YOU. If you're a team man, think you can do it, practice is tomorrow at lunch time.'

And so the following day we gathered in the school yard and were introduced to basketball. Two wooden boxes were set up at either end of the school yard. Our teacher said the first thing was, we needed two teams. Presumer Livingstone and Caruso Kelly got to pick. Then our teacher said we needed a catcher to stand on each box. I was made catcher for Caruso's team. It felt good up there. If I tapped my feet, I could hear the hollowness beneath me – like standing on a tin roof. And if you stood your feet at opposite corners of the box, you could rock it, imagine you were on a horse clip-clopping over the American prairie to take on the Red Indians. But the best part was feeling like a giant. You weren't high the way you might be in an aeroplane or if you were a bird, with everything tiny and hard to recognise. It was more like having suddenly grown three feet taller – like one of the darkie basketballers our teacher had talked about. You could see the tops of people's heads, and beyond the school yard to the chapel steps and the grotto on one side, the entrance to Jail Square away on the other, and out past the army camp in the middle, the hills looking purple and bruised. Even the air seemed clearer up on the box – above the sweat and stink of things.

The only problem was that, as well as being high up, you were wobbly. Falling off would be very easy. I thought about getting a couple of bits of wood to stick under the box, to steady it, but decided not to. There might be some rule that said you couldn't do that kind of thing. And if people saw me steadying it, they might think I was scared.

In basketball, our teacher explained, like someone who knew, each team had eleven players. Ten men out the field and one on the box – he was the catcher. And the job of every team was to get the ball to their catcher. To do that, you could run four steps, but after that you had to pass. It was a simple enough game. Our teacher hardly had to roar at us more than a couple times before we caught on to it. At the other end of the school yard, you could hear the fifth class teacher yelling at his team: 'Can you not count? Or is it deafness? Four steps. FOUR!'

That first day we had to stay all lunch time and then for

an hour when school had finished. Afterwards, we plodded home and compared how wet our necks were with sweat. On one thing we were all agreed: basketball was a smashing game, and we were going to give fifth class the pulverising of their life. The final practice before the game was set for Thursday after school. Walking down the school yard, we punched the air and leaped to catch and throw invisible balls. You could say we had caught basketball fever.

All except Cammy Grant, who walked with his fists in his trouser pockets and said it was a bollocks of a game. Because during the whole practice Cammy hadn't caught a single ball. All anybody had to do was stand beside him. Cammy was hopelessly out-classed – even the smallest of us was four feet tall. Mind you, he could stamp on your toes, and when he backed into you, he would whack his elbows into your stomach. But if you watched out for that, you were all right. By the time the practice had finished, Cammy was twitching with rage. Not that being a catcher was an easy job either. When the ball came my direction, I kept leaning too far forward and falling off the box.

'A frigging wee girls' game!' Cammy shouted, as we moved down the yard. 'Should give out ribbons for people's hair.'

'Shut up, Humpy,' Snowball Gallagher told him.

'You look over the convent wall – they never stop playing it. Even the bloody nun. I saw her one day – big black frock thing tucked up her knickers.' Cammy laughed harshly. 'Knickers are in the rules. Wait to you see – yous'll all have to bring in your mas' knickers.'

Cammy was sort of funny to listen to when he got worked up like that. And I suppose if you had to go round with a hump under your shirt, you'd feel angry too. Snowball Gallagher cheered things up by telling us about his sister who had two pairs of knickers – navy blue ones she wore to school, and shiny pink ones for going to *céilís*. Then everybody started saying how often they had seen knickers, and where their ma kept her knickers at night, and could a girl have a pee standing up? For a while we kind of forgot about basketball.

On Thursday morning during the break I was halfway up the fire-escape stairs to the storeroom with a crate of empty milk bottles in my hands. Our teacher gave it to a different boy each day, and today was my turn. As I passed the door of the fifth class, Andy Dunne came out. He closed the brass latch behind him carefully, then made a silent monkey leap that landed him right in front of me. Andy had mud-coloured eyes, and teeth with sharp edges that made me uneasy. He took the front of my Fair Isle pullover in his fist.

'Who told you to come up here?' Our teacher, I told him. He pushed me against the wall. 'You don't come up again except I say you can, hear me? If you do, you're for it.' His face was three inches from mine. I could see little bubbles of spittle between his crooked teeth. 'Are you playing in this basketball match against us?' I said I wasn't sure. 'Better not be. Because if you are, I'm going to break your face.'

As I sidled away he kicked the crate and made the bottles rattle.

At lunch time and in the afternoon everybody was talking, not about the basketball match, but about Woolworth's new shop. That morning, after weeks of preparation, it had opened. Presumer Livingstone said his ma had slept standing up, leaning against the main door, to be the first person in to get the bargains. Caruso Kelly said he knew a man that worked in the back of the place, and that Friday night he was going to open it up and pass out two dozen pairs of football boots to him and his brother.

'Woolworth's has no football boots,' Presumer said.

Caruso just rolled his eyes and said maybe it was high heel shoes then, he couldn't remember, but definitely either shoes or boots. Or gloves.

'Know what I heard?' Yo-Yo Farren said, his head nodding up and down as usual. 'They're giving away free toys after school today. They have this big room with toys up to the roof, and all you have to do is go and ask the man there and he has to give you whatever you want. It's the rule, until the room's empty. Starting after school today.'

Soon everybody was talking about the free toys at Woolworth's. The result was, at three o'clock nearly half our class went running in a crowd up the chapel steps, along George Street, down the Courthouse Hill and into Market Street to make sure they got their share of the toys. I was thinking of running after them myself, only then our teacher came out of the classroom and stared at us. So the twelve of us, including myself and Cammy Grant, waited in the yard to hear about tomorrow's game. Our teacher ran his hand through his hair and said, by crikey, picking this team would be no big job. He needed eleven men on a team and there were just twelve of us there. He'd save time if he simply picked the person who wasn't going to play.

Our teacher was really good at making his mind up. If he decided we were going to have a test, we got one. If he decided that we needed to do more singing, then we would have three different singing sessions every day until he decided we wouldn't. Picking the one person who wouldn't be on the team was nothing to him.

'Grant,' he said. 'Grant, I have a job for you. It's an important, responsible job, part of the teamwork. If somebody was to steal these coats, the boys playing could catch pneumonia. So we'll be depending on you.' Then he turned away, clapping his hands for us to gather our things and go straight home.

They say your ears get hot when somebody is saying bad things about you. In that case, our teacher's ears must have been roasting for the next fifteen minutes. All the way home Cammy never stopped – about our teacher, the way he walked, the way he talked, the sound of his laugh. He said our teacher could stick his coats where the monkey stuck the nuts, and put his basketball where the sun never shines.

So when on Friday at lunch time Cammy turned up in the school yard with the rest of us for the game, I was amazed. Was he here to show his silent contempt for our teacher? Or maybe he still had a dream of glory, thought he could maybe get picked, the teacher have some change of heart. Anyway, while we peeled off our coats and pretended to wrestle, Cammy sat at the playground edge, his humped back to us, lobbing small stones towards the school railings. Eventually the fifth class teacher stood in the middle of the yard, blew a whistle until we were all quiet, and announced that he would be the referee. Which showed you what his idea of fair was, given that his class was one of the two teams. I climbed up on my box, facing the fifth class catcher at the other end of the yard, and the rest lined up in the centre for the throw-in.

'Grant!' our teacher yelled at Cammy from the opposite side of the yard. 'Face the field of play, if that's not a lot of trouble. Now!'

'Thought you said for me to mind the coats, sir,' Cammy called over his shoulder in a muffled voice.

Our teacher took an angry step towards him, only then the fifth class teacher blew his whistle and raised his arm for attention. This game, he yelled, would have two halves, ten minutes each. We were to take no more than four steps with the ball. We were to throw it, not kick it. Anyone he got kicking the ball would be off the field quicker than a dose of salts through a duck. Understood? His cheeks bulged like apples as he blew the whistle.

From the start the fifth class took a grip on the game. They weren't good at passing – one of their team got hit on the back of the head by a pass. But their tackling was miles better than ours. They hunted in twos. The one in front would come at you with his fists, pretending to block the ball but actually punching your chest and face. While this was happening, the other one would spear his elbow into the softest part of your back that he could find. Knees smarting and kidneys aching, our play patterns got confused. Once one of us got the ball, he threw it – high, low, far, near – anywhere to get the fifth class assassins away from him. During the first part of the game we got into their half on just two occasions. And on both Andy Dunne, who was their fullback, jostled me off the box. Up there my snotter was safe, but not the rest. His shoulders thudded into my knees as hard as he could, even when the ball was at the other end; and once I felt his nails claw across my ankle. By half-time we were two goals down.

Our teacher gathered us around him at my box. 'What yous are,' he said quietly, like someone sharing a secret, 'is a pack of bloody girls. Jooking about, scared of your shadow, bloody sickening, wee girls.'

'My knee, sir – look!' Snowball Gallagher was holding up his knee and hopping about. 'And they left lumps on my back!'

Our teacher's lips were shaking and his face was dark red. 'And why didn't you bury your boot in one of them, then?' Nobody spoke. Reaching into his bag, he produced six oranges and a penknife. 'Get these into yous,' he said. 'For energy.' He sliced the oranges in half and passed them round.

We stood there panting and sucking, afraid to speak. There was a half orange left over. Our teacher walked across the yard to where Cammy sat and dropped it in his lap. 'Now, Grant,' he told him, 'you're as entitled as any. Have a suck on that.'

Cammy looked at him, looked at the half orange thoughtfully, then lifted it and flicked it over the railings behind him into the long grass. Our teacher stared at Cammy for a moment, then back to the resting players; he seemed to wobble between the two of us. At that moment the fifth class teacher gave a blast on his whistle. Finally, waving both arms in the air at once, our teacher shouted, 'Come on, come on, shake yourselves!' Then under his breath, when we had gathered round him: 'Pulverise the buggers, would you?'

Goose-pimply with determination, we took up our places.

Well of course we pulverised nobody. They were bigger than us and more ruthless. But we did begin to survive their rush-and-crush tactics. We did step aside as tackles came in. We did start to look up before throwing. We did move into space to receive passes. The only thing we didn't do – couldn't do – was score.

Afterwards some people tried to say it was my fault, but it wasn't. I leaned forward, I leaned back. I shouted for a pass, I shut up. No difference. Each time the ball came near, Andy Dunne was down on me like a threshing machine. Nails clawing, knees hefting, he had one intention: to bring me off that box. He succeeded, too. I had a choice between grabbing at the ball and landing on my face, or forgetting about the ball and using my hands to break my fall. I wanted to be heroic, but my body kept opting for staying in one piece.

And then, with five minutes to go, a chance. Wanger Duncan got the ball. He rocked back on his heels, took four quick steps and dummied a throw. Then with two fifth classers groping hopelessly, he lobbed an arcing pass that came at me out of the sky. It seemed to take an hour dropping, growing bigger and bigger as it came, straight towards my outstretched hands. For once, it seemed, I could show what I was made of.

But it didn't happen. At the same instant my hands closed on the ball Andy Dunne's body struck. The last time I'd looked he'd been nowhere around. But now he must have hurled himself straight at me. My legs went up in the air and my face, the other end of a seesaw, went down to the ground. In a crimson flash the playground exploded against my mouth. Somewhere a thousand miles away I felt the ball bobble from my hands, bounce gently, roll to a stop. I'd dropped it.

'Aagh!' Our teacher was standing over me, passing me a big hanky, then guiding my hand to my mouth. My face seemed to have got knocked out of order and someone had sewn a sausage into my lower lip. 'Stand up now, you'll be all right. Hup now.' I shook my head, blinking away tears. If I stood up, my mouth would fall off.

Our teacher's face got very red. With clenched fists he strode over to Cammy. 'Get up there and catch everything that comes within a mile of you. If you don't, you and me'll be having a cosy chat.'

Cammy had been to enough pictures to know what must happen next. Without removing his jacket (was there a hole in his shirt for the hump?), he climbed onto the box, smiling like Roy Rogers. His time had come.

What made Cammy different from me as a catcher was his centre of gravity. Lower, you see. Harder to knock over. Andy Dunne jostled and thumped at Cammy until his muddy eyes were bloodshot with trying, but he couldn't dislodge him. Cammy braced his sturdy little legs, bent forward from the waist and stayed on the box. Within a couple of minutes of restarting, a Wanger Duncan pass hit Cammy on the chest. Before it could bounce away, he'd reached out and held it. 2–1. Five minutes later a lob, this time from Snowball Gallagher. Cammy pushed one hand into Andy Dunne's face, took the catch with the other. We were level.

Behind me, our teacher was jumping in the air and growling. Even though it hurt my sausage lip, I found myself screaming encouragement through my hanky. We were on the brink of beating the fifth years.

And then we did it. My skin still crawls with pleasure when I remember it. Snowball Gallagher missed a pass, Wanger Duncan stretched and picked it up, he sent Presumer Livingstone away on his own up the left wing. Presumer's dummy wasn't all that good, but it fooled Andy Dunne. Turning, convinced that the ball was on its way, Dunne flung himself at Cammy – a repeat of the tackle that had taken me out. Only Cammy wasn't me. His legs didn't go flying up or his face down. Instead, with his left leg firm in the middle of the box, his right leg rose, almost elegantly, in defence. Flying in at full stretch, Andy was brought to a sudden stop against Cammy's raised knee. Like a half-empty bag of potatoes, Andy's body folded in two. Cammy shuddered for a moment, then lowered his right leg again. On the ground beside the box Andy lay curled, wheezing between coughs.

Cammy seemed barely to notice him. All his attention was on Presumer, who still had the ball. 'Throw it, Livingstone, before the bugger gets up!'

Presumer threw. Cammy held. And almost immediately the fifth class teacher, looking a bit fed up, blew his whistle. Our teacher ran forward, grabbed Cammy off the box and hugged him. Kept on hugging him for at least half a minute, his arms meeting just below Cammy's hump. Swung him round so that Cammy's little feet wobbled in the air. Finally, panting, he put him down.

'By God, you're a topper, Grant,' our teacher said, eyes wide and waving his hands like tambourines. 'And so's every one of you. Pure absolute top-of-the-drawer toppers. Now remember, training starts at lunch time on Tuesday. We want to be ready for the next competition.'

'Sir, that big ball is very slippy for catching,' Snowball Gallagher said. 'I have a wee ball at home. Can we use a wee-er ball, sir?'

'The ball is perfect – sure didn't you win?'

'But sir, we could play them again and beat them by even more.'

Our teacher's smile widened and he looked at each of our sweating faces in turn. 'Of course you could. You could beat them a hundred times over, but what would be the point of that? No, men. Time to widen our sporting range.' He put a fatherly hand on top of Cammy's head as he spoke. 'There's more to sport than just ball games. Think of athletics. Think of hammer-throwing and javelin.' He leaned down and stared into Cammy's face. 'And the best of the whole bunch, the high jump!' He rubbed his hands together at the thought. 'The fifth class teacher and me have got sticks and bar for it, so that's what we'll take them on at next week. The high jump. All right, everybody? All right, Grant?'

Cammy's face, still sweaty, had turned a bit white. Panting, he looked up at our teacher, then nodded. And there was a kind of recognition in that nod. Like Cammy himself, our teacher didn't bother much with rules.

HEATHER AND THE RELIC

SAMMY MCILWAINE'S SISTER LOOKED A LOT LIKE HIM – same fair hair, freckled face, slightly bulging blue eyes. The difference was that where Sammy's teeth were crooked, Heather's were neat. And where Sammy's shoulders were square and knocked you against walls when you walked beside him, Heather's were smooth and plump and pushed against the inside of her dress. If you looked carefully, you could see the little squares of thread in her frock being strained away from each other. Sometimes when she and Sammy climbed the barbed-wire fence to play with me, I'd picture how Heather's shoulders would look without the dress. When that happened, my skull felt that tickle you get when you suck lemonade too fast through a straw. 'Think of the thing you most enjoy doing and multiply it by a million million,' Brother Bozo would tell us when he was explaining what heaven would be like. I used to close my eyes and think of tumbling around in a barn full of Heather's shoulders.

The time I'm talking about, Heather and I were eleven; her brother Sammy, although in the same class as Heather, was twelve. All that year Brother Bozo made our class come in on Saturday mornings to do extra sums and writing for the eleven-plus exam. If I got the exam, I'd be able to go to the grammar school, where they wore blazers and had two handball alleys. If I failed, I'd go into sixth class and leave school at fourteen. When I complained about homework, my mother reminded me how awful a lifetime of carrying bricks in London would be, with a drip on my nose and the cold putting cracks in my knuckles.

At last, one Friday in February, with the sky bruised and threatening snow, the Head Brother came into our classroom. We stood and wished Brother Cahill a good afternoon in Irish. He was a tall bald man with eyebrows joined together in the middle. When he blew his nose, he folded his hanky over carefully and put it away in his pocket without even glancing at the contents. Now he stood at the front of the class, looking at us through his rimless glasses.

'Tráthnóna maith, a bhuachaillí. Afternoon, boys. Hands, now: Monday is . . . correct, well done. Eleven-plus day. Do or die, make-or-break day. Some of you will pass your examination; more of you will not. The way of the world and God's will, mysteries that are beyond our comprehension. But will I tell you what God will not do? He'll not fail a boy for trying. He will not. There's only one thing the Almighty will be death on. He will be death on – *I* will be death on – any boy not prepared to do his best. The boy who sits staring out the window, the boy who draws wee men or daggers at the bottom of his exam page. That's the boy our heavenly Father will be death on.' The Head Brother took a deep breath through his long straight nose. 'Hell for leather!' he shouted suddenly and loudly. 'That's how you must go for fifty minutes. And any boy who's not prepared to, let him be a man and pull out now, for he's not worth his salt and could not have God's blessing.' He paused and stared around the class. 'Very well. Now, stand, hands joined . . . Very good. Let us offer three Hail Marys for all those boys on Monday prepared to go at things with a heart and a half.'

Afterwards, Brother Cahill announced in a quieter voice that on Saturday *The Song of Bernadette* would be on in Miller's Picture House. 'Not Jane Russell, not Tarzan the Ape Man. Just the blessed Saint Bernadette, virgin and martyr, resisting evil as an example to us all. At half the normal price.'

Heather and Sammy didn't hear Brother Cahill. They went to the Protestant school with the flag outside it on the other side of the town. Because he had trouble with sums and writing, Sammy had been kept back a year. He wasn't doing the eleven-plus; Heather was. It'd be nice, I thought, that she'd be sitting in her school on Monday, sucking a pencil the same time as me. I'd seen Heather sucking a stick of rock and she had nice lips.

'Our teacher's head's a marley,' Sammy said. 'He's put George Watson in for the eleven-plus, even though he thinks pygmies live at the North Pole. I'm miles better than Watson.'

George Watson was a tall sullen boy who helped carry a banner every Twelfth of July. Once he had stood on a step above me at the town library and asked if I would like him to bust my snotter.

'Poor George,' Heather said. 'He gets confused.'

'Your head's a marley too,' Sammy said, jostling her with his shoulder.

On Friday evening we climbed into our den in the hay shed. Lying there on our stomachs, with the straw pricking through our clothes, I told Sammy and Heather about *The Song of Bernadette*, and what Brother Bozo had told us about her. 'It was only when she was nearly dead that people would believe a word out of her, and then they all came round and said they were sorry and cried. Brother Bozo was in her house two years ago in France – he says the place is full of crutches. Left there by cured people.'

'Buck stupid people, more like it,' Sammy said. 'They could have took the .crutches home and played high jump. If they were all that cured.' The way Sammy talked sometimes wasn't right, even for a Protestant. He had once said Our Lady couldn't be a Blessed Virgin because she went to the toilet.

Heather pushed a strip of fair hair behind her ear and smiled at me. 'I'd love a pair of crutches. You could have your name carved on them.' It was hard to tell if she meant my name or hers.

I suggested, very casually, that the three of us might go to *The Song of Bernadette*. The truth was, my mother never let me go to the pictures on my own. Besides, you never knew, Sammy and Heather might be converted after seeing the miracles. CONEYWARREN BOY CONVERTS PROTESTANT PAIR, the *Ulster Herald* would say. The Pope might even send me a medal.

Heather said she would definitely like to go. Sammy made a face and said it didn't sound much. He preferred cowboy pictures or comedies. In the end Heather convinced him that there might be dancing as well as singing in the Bernadette picture. 'Cripples all jumping on tables and that after they get better. Like Gene Kelly and them,' she told him. Sammy really liked film stars who danced on tables. He'd even tried it once or twice at home, according to Heather. We agreed we'd meet outside Miller's for the matinée at half-two.

Only then, on Saturday at one o'clock, Sammy and Heather's uncle from Ballymena visited them. 'Who's getting to be a quare big wee girl?' he asked Heather, smiling and nipping her first on the cheek and then on the bum. He always did that. Then he took her and Sammy on the bus to see the latest Roy Rogers picture in Dromore, a town ten miles away. Which left me stuck with nobody to go to *The Song of Bernadette* with.

My mother was in the kitchen, rubbing a mop over the cream-coloured tiles. I drank a cup of water from the tap. Made a piece of bread and jam and chewed it moodily. Sigh-ed and stood staring out the kitchen window, whistling. At last she stopped working and asked me if something was wrong. I told her about Heather and Sammy's uncle.

Her mouth was tight as she leaned on the mop. 'Some people,' she said, 'think more of an oul' cowboy than a good saint. Though God help them, I suppose. They are what they are.'

I bit my lip and wished in my heart God had made me a Protestant too, if that's what it took to get to the pictures.

Maybe she noticed. Because suddenly she put down the mop, pounded upstairs and came back carrying a glass disc the size of a half-crown. I'd seen it before in her wardrobe. It had cardboard backing and a tiny piece of material under the glass. 'It's a relic,' she said, holding it out. 'A wee snip of the dress Saint Bernadette was wearing the day she died.' It was hard even to recognise it as material, except for the tiny edges of thread. My mother removed one of the half-dozen safety pins that were fastened to the front of her pinafore, and began attaching the relic to my jersey. 'For to guide and protect you through every question in Monday's exam. None of your cowboys could do that.'

Immediately I felt panic. Could I not keep it up my sleeve? I asked. Supposing I met somebody – supposing I ran into George Watson! He'd bust my snotter and my relic.

When she saw the shine of tears in my eyes, she relented.

'Fix it inside to your vest, then, Jimmy son. Carefully.' She pulled up my jersey. 'You could have no better thing against your skin than a bit of Saint Bernadette.'

The following day after dinner I was playing handball by myself against the boilerhouse wall and wishing Sunday was over when Sammy and Heather climbed the fence. Sammy landed heavily, heels thudding into the grass, Heather with a little bounce. The singing cowboy, they declared, had been brilliant. Roy Rogers had sung 'Home on the Range' and the baddy had screamed and fallen over a cliff at the end.

'We'll go to the hay shed,' Sammy said. 'Pee-ko! Pee-ko!' Firing and ducking, he ran ahead of us. Heather and I followed, smiling at each other.

We turned the wildcat on the hay shed rafters for half an hour, with Heather's hair and dress hanging upside down for a second, as she panted to complete the head-over-heels in the air. Then we went trapping spiders in a matchbox. At the back of the byre we cornered a hen and pulled three feathers from its wing for being Indians with. We would have fished for minnows but when we got down to the river there were none. On the way back Heather found a frog in a clump of long grass, and luckily Sammy had both a hanky and string in his pocket ('I always carry them'). So we were able to tie a hanky to the frog and take turns dropping it from a tree and pretending it was a parachutist. After the frog had been dropped from the second-highest branch, Sammy said he was going home to see what was for the tea. I was still up the tree, watching the top of Heather's head below me, where she was trying to fold the dead frog's arms across its chest. And as I watched the nice straight middle parting and the way her hair frothed up on either side of it, I felt the bubbles in my head. Suddenly it was clear, beyond any hint of doubt, what I must do, whatever the consequences. I scrambled down, put a hand on her shoulder – her lovely shoulder – and spoke quietly. 'Come behind the henhouse till I show you something.'

Without hesitation she tossed the frog's corpse into a clump of nettles, wiped her hands on her dress and followed me. In the shadow of the henhouse we hunkered down, listening to the sound of cluckings and soft complainings from inside it. A hen appeared round the corner, stood on one leg, yellow eye watching us. I nudged Heather. 'Bet you never seen one of these.' Slowly I pulled up my jersey.

The effect was immediate. Her eyes bulged even wider, her lower lip hung open.

'When Saint Bernadette was in bed dying, she wore this. So when you're sick you rub yourself with it and you get better. Or if you want something,' I said.

Heather leaned closer. 'Like Aladdin,' she said. 'What's the glass bit for?'

'That's to keep the relic safe.' I paused, willed myself to go on. 'Swapsy for four kisses.' She looked away. I spoke carefully. 'If you swear you'll give me it back, you can have this during the eleven-plus.' I paused. 'If you let me kiss you four times.'

She turned to look at me, her eyes as blue as Our Lady's dress. Then she took a twig and started drawing on the ground.

'Four?'

'Yes. Four kisses.'

'Here, do you mean? Beside the hens?'

'Nobody's about.'

She was silent for a minute. Then, 'On the face, d'you mean?'

I swallowed. 'No. The . . . the shoulder. You see, Heather,' I spoke as fast as I could, in case I'd lose my nerve and stop, 'you've got lovely shoulders. I'm a slave to your shoulders. They're so pushy.'

She glanced towards me again, said, 'Mmm.'

What was the hold-up? She was a Protestant, wasn't she? They could do whatever they wanted.

At last she smiled. 'I've decided.' A bead of sweat dribbled down my rib cage. 'No shoulders.' She stood, hands on hips, a little blue vein disappearing into the plumpness of her throat. 'Shoulders are silly. Nobody in the pictures kisses shoulders, except maybe a cowboy with his horse.' She stared at me, little teeth showing, looking like Grace Kelly, only smaller and a good bit fatter. 'But I don't mind my b.t.m.'

The sweat on my ribs turned to ice. Had she really said that?

'Just looking, I mean. Nothing else. No kissing.' She stood and threw the twig as far as she could. 'You've never seen a girl's b.t.m., have you?' I shook my head, humble, inexperienced. 'Right, then. Turn round and close your eyes.'

I turned away, eyelids squeezed shut. How had things got to this point? I hadn't really wanted this to happen. Her shoulders had been what haunted my thoughts, not her, her... There was a rustling, followed by the sound of something falling to the ground. A shoe? Then, 'You can open now.'

She was lying on the ground on her stomach, peering over her shoulder to check that I had opened my eyes. Her legs lay stretched behind her, straight and tight together, with the hem of her frock covering down to the back of her knees. She buried her face in her hands. Her voice was muffled. 'When I say one, two, three, lift the skirt and look. Once you've lifted I'll count to five, then you must turn away and close your eyes again. Promise? Right. One, two, three. Lift!'

What amazed me most was, it looked familiar. I'd seen it before, in a dream maybe, or on a riverbank on a hot August day. Not this bum but one like it, smiling up at me, pink and terrifying. Before she got to the count of five I had turned away again, eyes screwed shut, light dancing behind my lids.

A minute later I passed her the relic. 'You'll see,' I said, my mouth dry. 'Saint Bernadette will help you with the questions.'

'Okey-dokey.' She jumped to her feet and ran twinkling towards the fence, her hair streaming behind her in a small comet tail.

'I'll get it back after the exam – at your school!' I shouted, as she paused to hitch her skirt before clambering over the wire.

She waved without looking back.

Next day, when our answers had been collected and we'd rubbed our cramped hands, Brother Cahill came in. Dabbed the end of his nose with his hanky, then shoved it up his sleeve. Now, he said. We were to put all thought of the exam business clean out of our heads. Take our lunch time now even though it was only quarter to twelve, but make no mistake about being back for one o'clock. Now all stand for three Hail Marys to the Blessed Virgin for her gracious help.

I walked down the main street towards the Protestant school, my mind raw and stripped like a rabbit I'd seen once hanging in a butcher's window. The exam had been not too hard, but I had kept having periods of whirling, stripy confusion. When I closed my eyes to work out twelve times seven, or what house number was sixteen down from number eleven and on the other side of the street, Heather's bum kept appearing. Not as it had actually been but a shining version, like the apostles' faces when they came down the mountain after being transfigured. It glowed at me while an invisible choir sang very high notes for minutes on end, before I was able to force my eyes open again and push on with the exam. Ears burning, I whispered aspirations to Saint Bernadette and wrote down door numbers that could have been right or wrong. With ten minutes to go, I still had nine questions to answer. Breathing hard, I flew through them. There was no time left to check over anything.

At the school gates she was waiting. Eyes, excited blue, teeth begging to be sucked.

'It was easy-peasy, wasn't it? Twangerdick warned us not to waste a minute, but it was easy. I was finished the second in my row.'

I nodded, kicked a stone, began to say something about door numbers.

She mustn't have heard. 'Da-da, dah–dah–dah–dah–*dah*!' she sang, holding her hands above her head and doing a little dance on the pavement.

I said in a dignified way that I'd like the relic back now.

She paused, knee in midair. Oh, right, the whatsit, the relic. The thing was, she'd given it to George Watson. No, no, not given. Lent it to him. That was all. 'He looked so sad before the exam. Nerves, poor pet. So I slipped it from under my jumper and gave it to him. Lent it.' She laughed. 'He said he could feel it still warm from being up my jumper!'

My heart, free-falling, shot past my stomach and crumpled against the soles of my feet. 'George Watson has the relic?'

'No, no, no, no, no, no!' Her hands fluttered in the air as if rubbing out my words. 'Not now. But yes, he *did* have it. There was a sort of mix-up after the exam, you see. George came up to me in the yard after it was over, and really, such a state! Waving his fist, shouting, you know, bad words. Said the whatsit had muddled his brains. He had been doing great, he said, and then he began to think about it in his trouser pocket, and he started getting this, this *pain* in his, you know, and he couldn't remember things the teacher had said, about how to do out numbers and colours and all that stuff, to stop getting mixed up. And next thing, he took it out of his pocket, the whatsit, in the middle of the playground, and said it was a bloody Fenian charm. And before I could stop him' – she touched my sleeve briefly, gently – 'he had it threw over the wall of the boys' lavs!' She paused. 'But I did grand, even without it. And George will get it back for you, bet you he will, if you just ask him. Poor dote gets that worked up.' A handbell clanged behind her. 'Oh my flipping goodness, the time's up. Bye-bye!' A final wriggle of her shoulders and she was gone.

I walked slowly back to my own school – past Miller's Picture House, up the hill, past the Protestant church, past our own chapel. My mother had given me a sixpence that morning, along with the relic, to steady my nerves. Fortunately I hadn't used it. At the café down the street from our school I went in and bought a bag of chips. They were so hot I had to curl my lips away when biting on them. I was so busy I didn't notice Sammy McIlwaine until he jumped down from the wall outside the bank.

'Give us a chip, greedygorb,' he panted, shouldering me against the wall of Boyce's newspaper shop. 'Forgot my lunch and Twangerdick let me home for it, only then our Ma was gone out and now I'm half-starved.' His hand, plump and pink, grabbed two more chips. 'What're you doing up here?'

'Looking for my relic.'

Sammy nodded – Heather must have told him about it. But not the bit about the b.t.m., or Sammy wouldn't be so friendly.

A solution began to take shape in my head. 'Know who took it?' I said. 'George Watson.'

'That blurt. He thinks Eskimos live in New Zealand.'

'He took it from your Heather and threw it over the lavs at your school. For nothing.'

'He wanted my football boots one time. I told him he could have them up his arse. You eating all those?'

'Take two. Listen.' I had it worked out. 'Would you like all of these?' A chip half in and half out of his mouth, he looked at me. 'I need you to help us find the relic first. In your school lavs.'

'OK. Give us the chips.'

'Search first.'

Sammy said it'd be best to go in the back way, in case Twangerdick or some of the other teachers saw us. I gave him a leg up, the chips rolled up tight and stuck deep in my trouser pocket, then he pulled me over the back wall of the lavs. Like cat burglars we jumped down inside. The lavs had ten slate urinals and three cubicles without doors. The bowls were streaked with different shades of brown, and the smell was like at our school.

'Which one did he throw it into?'

'Don't know.'

For fifteen minutes we prowled through the cubicles. We looked in and behind the lav bowls, we peered along the shallow stream of urine that ran the length of the slate stalls. We even peered into the cracks in the wall above the stalls, in case it had got lodged there. Nothing. It was only when we'd given up and were walking back towards the wall that we found it. It lay at the foot of a tree, as if placed there carefully by someone, the little scrap of material gazing up like a tiny eye.

'Is it still working?' Sammy asked as I picked it up.

'I think so.' I breathed on the glass bit and polished it on my sleeve.

'That Watson is some blurt. Give us the chips.'

When I got home, I lied to my mother. The relic had been a great comfort, I told her. When I was working out twelve times seven or what house the Smith family lived in, all I had to do was stare at the relic and the answer came! She looked pleased when I said that. When I went to confession on Saturday, I told Father Brennan everything. My bargain with Heather, the lies to my mother, everything. You have to, if you want to get rid of your sins.

In the dark on the other side of the lattice grille he shifted and sighed. I could smell the tobacco smoke from his clothes. God, he said, would sort things out in the end. I could rest assured about that. But from now on, and for the rest of my life too, did I hear? I was to steer clear of bargains and agreements about girls' underwear. If I didn't I'd land in serious bother, serious sin. Did I hear now? I said I did. He gave me three decades of the rosary. It was my personal worst for a penance.

Two months later the eleven-plus results came out. Father Brennan had been right – God did sort everything. I passed, Heather failed, and George Watson, who by then had moved to England with his mother, got the lowest fail mark that any boy had ever got in the history of the exam. Or that's what Sammy McIlwaine claimed. He said it had been in the *Tyrone Constitution*.

Heather rolled her eyes. 'Poor George,' she said, slipping her finger under the neckline of her dress and scratching herself gently. 'I feel sorry for him.'

'You would,' said Sammy, shouldering her against the boilerhouse wall. 'What about that time he wanted you to do the thing with your knickers, only you wouldn't? He's a right dirty blurt.'

Heather bent down to fix the buckle of her sandal, saying nothing. When she finally straightened up her face was red, and her neck too. 'Poor George,' she said again, softly.

DIRTY PICTURES

HOLLYWOOD FIRST TOUCHED MY LIFE WHEN I WAS EIGHT. I knew there were pictures on in the town every night, at Miller's Picture House. Presumer Livingstone told me coorting couples fought each other, scrabbing and kicking, to see who would get sitting in the double seats at the back. I'd even been through the peeled green doors once, with Anne and my mother, at a film about the lepers and Damian. Mammy made the three of us sit in the front row – we'd be closer to the miracles there, she said. That was the only time I remember her ever going to the pictures. But she knew what she didn't like. 'Muck and dirt,' she would repeat, nodding her head. If pressed, she'd admit that the Damian film or *The Song of Bernadette* were all right. But the whole shebang of the others were about nothing only muck and dirt and ones committing sin, as far as she could see. Besides, no child should be trotting the road after half-ten at night. When I grew up, I promised myself, I would live beside the pictures. Inside the picture house itself, if they would let me. Meantime, my evenings limped by, surrounded by hens and cows and grass. When boys in school mentioned Johnny Weissmuller's chest or Betty Grable's legs, I sniggered and tried to look knowing.

Then on a September day in 1951, to a fanfare of publicity, Miller's Picture House moved into the sun. For a number of months past, it explained in the local paper, patrons had been petitioning management to reconsider hours of opening. In response to these persistent pleas it was happy to announce that from this week, all motion pictures would have two houses – the first house commencing at 6 p.m., the second commencing at 8.30 p.m. Miller's Picture House thanked its patrons in anticipation, and looked forward to welcoming us to an extended schedule in their luxurious premises.

That afternoon Anne was waiting for me in the shadow of the school wall. Normally she walked home ahead of me, because the convent got off twenty minutes before the Brothers. But today she was waiting.

'Here,' she said, and gave me a bite of her toffee apple without my even having to ask.

Then, bulging schoolbags strapped on our backs, we trudged past the chapel, down the hill, as far as Swann and Mitchell's shoe shop.

'Cross,' she said.

At the other side of the street the green door was covered in a yellow handbill, like an advertisement for Duffy's Circus. We stood back and considered it.

'About flipping time,' Anne said. I knew from experience not to say anything – she would go on in a minute. 'This dump is miles behind everywhere else. In New York the pictures start before people even get up.'

'Before everybody gets up? Who goes, then?'

'Cripples,' Anne said quickly. 'Their crutches take up that much room they go early. Two seats each, one for the cripple, one for the crutches.' She pointed to the poster again. 'Six p.m. it starts for the first house. And eight thirty, the second.' She chewed at her lower lip. 'Say it takes ten minutes to get first-house people out, and ten minutes to get second-house people in. That's twenty minutes.'

'And say another five minutes for coorting couples to fight for the back seats,' I added.

Anne looked hard at me. 'Fight?'

'Presumer Livingstone saw them. Elbowing and scrabbing.'

She nipped my arm, but not as hard as she could have. Her voice was like coke under a door. 'Presumer Livingstone has a smell off him would choke a horse.' She turned back to the poster. 'We'd be on our way home by twenty past eight. Nowhere near dark at twenty past eight.'

'One night it wasn't dark at one o'clock in the morning,' I told her. 'I looked out and there was a moon.'

Anne scanned the lower half of the notice. 'They've got a picture with songs in it.'

That sounded good. Presumer said that when Roy Rogers played his guitar at the end and sang with the horse going along at the same time, clippety-clop, yodel-ay-ee-ho, he felt like cheering. I asked her if the songs would be cowboy songs.

'Wouldn't be a bit surprised. Not one bit.' She looked at me with her eyes narrowed, as if she was thinking about something. 'We could be home before nine o'clock,' she said at last. 'Earlier if we ran the whole of the lane.'

'Home from where?'

'The *pictures*. Did you not hear me saying that?'

'But we're not allowed go to the pictures.'

Anne took a grip of my hair in her hand and stared into my face. 'That was *before*. Savvy, Gringo Jimbo? It's different now. They've changed the times. It says it on the frigging poster.'

I checked where the sun was streaming down onto the war

monument in the middle of the Courthouse Hill. 'If we leave now, we'll be home years before it gets dark.'

This time Anne's nip was like a pair of pliers. 'Would you *listen*? Home from the pictures. I'm talking about being home before dark *from the frigging pictures*.'

A boy rode by on a messenger bike. 'How's my wee fatty Annie?' he called.

Anne stuck out her tongue at him, but smiled even before he'd passed. It wasn't until he had parked his bike and gone into Gallagher's grocer's that she turned to me again. 'Look, Dim Jim. The pictures start at six. Right? If we go to the pictures at six, we'll be home ages before dark. Right?'

'Do we not have to ask, then?'

She adjusted her schoolbag on her back, gestured for me to follow her back up the hill. 'All depends. We'll just have to wait and see. Now don't ask any more questions. I'm thinking.'

All the way home she went on thinking. When we reached the turn in our long, L-shaped lane, she said that she had finished thinking and that we would now run for the house. Since she was older than me, she had already finished and gone inside by the time I came gasping, exhausted, into the yard. Not even the hens picking around the gate bothered to jump out of my way.

The kitchen was dark after the bright afternoon sun. 'I'm home,' I announced.

Anne was seated at the table. 'I already told her we were home,' she said.

'Doesn't mean I can't say it too.'

'No, only it's stupid, because Mammy knows already.'

Mammy levered herself upright in the armchair by the cooker where she'd been dozing, and sighed. We were home.

She'd made stew, potatoes and cabbage for our dinner. And semolina with a bull's-eye of jam in the middle, which I ate around and kept until last. Usually when Mammy asked how we'd got on at school, Anne would complain between mouthfuls. There were girls who smelt, or teachers who slapped people for nothing, or lunches she'd been given that were too small. Today, though, was different. Today she talked about the goal she'd scored in hockey practice, about one of the nuns who was dying but didn't care because it meant she'd be in heaven quicker, and about a black rabbit she said we'd seen in the field at the road. We'd seen nothing of the sort. I had my mouth open to deny every word of her story when she showed her clenched teeth and shook her head a tiny bit in warning. I was to say nothing. When Mammy gave us a sweet each from a bag she had hid in her apron, Anne gave her a big smile and said 'Thank you, Mammy' three times. Even our mother was looking at her a bit funny.

Afterwards, when we were clearing the table and carrying the dishes to the scullery, I whispered to her, 'What about the pictures?'

She pushed against me with her shoulder so that I nearly dropped the four plates I was carrying. 'Do you want to go to the pictures or not?'

'I do.'

'And do you want to ask the right way or the wrong way?'

'The right way.'

'Then leave the frigging planning to me, would you? And less halfwit questions.'

'You,' I whispered. 'You never stop asking damn questions yourself.'

She tried to kick at me, but she wasn't able to with the handful of cups she was carrying.

I had no homework to do so I went out to play. There was a blackbird walking around the flowerbed at the bottom of the lawn. Very carefully I lifted a stone but even before my arm was drawn back to throw, the bird had shot away into the nearby trees. So I practised jumping over the flowerbed for a while, keeping a watch out of the side of my eye in case he was sitting on a branch within hitting distance. No luck. He was probably flying home this minute with a mouthful of worms for his babies. Spear beak stabbing into wee soft worms. I felt slightly sick.

I had landed in the flowerbed for the third time when she came out. *The elegant Lady Anna moved smiling through the rose garden.* She pretended not to see me and started bouncing a tennis ball against the wall.

'So are we going?'

'Going where?' The ball described a great loop, giving her time to turn around before catching it.

'The pictures.'

'I thought you said we weren't allowed to the pictures.' She did a tricky clap-turn-clap-and-catch movement as she spoke.

'Are we allowed or not, for flip's sake?'

'Mind your tongue, Mr Mac. Mammy says yes and you're to get the money off Daddy.' Then with a contemptuous nod that sent light glistening through her hair, she disappeared indoors again.

Sir Jim inspected his elegant cuffs as he moved towards the Duke's study. The holes in the boilerhouse wall gaped like eye sockets as I squelched towards the byre. On the midden heap opposite, a glum hen picked its way in search of nourishment. It stopped, one foot curled in midair as Father's voice yelled a threat: the cross cow was giving bother. Then, as the rip of milk into the bucket resumed, the hen went on searching.

He was in a corner stall, half-crouched under the cow's belly. A quick check to confirm his grip on the tits, then he continued his work while staring at me. His bottom teeth were loose and stuck out a bit. I prodded a piece of caked dung with my wellington. If I hadn't the words put together in my head I could have been stuck.

'Daddy, Mammy says we can go to the pictures if you say yes and can we have the money?'

He went on milking for several beats. 'Money?'

'For the pictures.'

'Pictures?' It was as if I'd said 'fairies' or 'tigers'. 'Is the hens fed and their eggs collected?'

I nodded. I hadn't an idea if they were or not, but I knew what no would mean.

'And the eggs cleaned and packed? Mind, the eggs has to be got ready for Doherty's tomorrow, first thing.'

'They are. They're done.' No reason or motive can excuse a lie. Sorry, God. Sorry sorry sorry.

He turned his stare to the brimming bucket between his knees as if counting the bubbles. I stood on the empty toe of my left wellington and thought desperately how my right foot was bigger than my left. I was deformed.

'Can we go then, Daddy?' I asked softly. 'Mammy says we can go if you say we can.'

'How much are you looking?'

'One-and-six. Um, each. Three shillings altogether for me and Anne.'

'My God Almighty.' He set the bucket on the floor, protecting it from a sudden kick with one hand. Dipped into his trouser pocket with the other. 'Here. Take the three shillings out of that. Before I change my mind.'

His big sausage fingers crossed the groop, cradling change.

I approached and carefully picked out a half-crown, a thruppence and three pennies. *The smiling Earl slid a bag of sovereigns across the polished desk. 'Now, young feller-m'lad!'*

'Have you got it?'

'I have. Thank you, Daddy.' I moved towards the door and behind me the rhythm of squirting milk started up again. I rolled my eyes to heaven. Thank you, God. Even as the prayer sounded in my head, the thruppenny bit slid through my fingers into the liquid mess in the groop. It vanished completely.

'*Shite.*' I stopped, frozen in a slightly bent position.

'What'd you say? What'd you do?' I could feel his head re-emerged from behind the cow's caked flank. He knew immediately. 'Did you drop it? Did you drop the good money in the cow dung?'

'No. I – I only dropped thruppence. It was slippy...'

'You dropped thruppence in the groop!' The cross cow gave a half-hearted kick and he hammered at her with his fist. 'Stand up, you brute!' Then he pointed at the groop, his finger jabbing in emphasis. 'If you dropped it, then get down there and get it out this minute.'

I made vague gestures towards the stinking drain, like a diver trying to get courage to step off the board.

'On your hands and knees, man. Roll up your sleeve and hoke about till you get it.' He had half-risen from his stool and his voice burned like a hot poker. 'Or do I have to take a *stick* to you?'

I began to whimper, and crouched over the mess.

'Roll up that sleeve – on up, on up yet. If you'd watched what you were at, you'd have less bother now.' He'd stopped shouting, but his voice had an unbreakable insistence.

He watched till my hand entered. Then, after a full final

few tugs under the cow, he left with the frothing bucket.

The warm brown closed over my wrist, then my arm, and I began to bawl. Softly at first, in case he heard me. When I was sure he was gone, I roared my humiliation. 'I can't find it – it's not here. Aha, ahaaaaaaaah!' The cross cow twisted its head and looked back at me, alarmed. 'Bloody oul' bugger, damn you for shite. This is your fault.' It wasn't, of course, but I needed something to blame. 'Aha, ahaaaaah. I caaan't fi-i-i-nd it.'

Neither I could. The thruppenny bit seemed to have melted into the mess. There was nothing on the bottom but smooth stone floor. I close my fist and shivered as dung squirted through my fingers. Nothing but grains of corn and straw.

Five minutes later, sweating and snuffling, my face feeling twice the normal size, I located it. There must have been a current in the groop or something, because it had moved at least four inches to the left of where it had entered. Giving my arm a gentle shake, I lifted it clear. Wailed louder than ever when I saw the steaming stocking of brown that had been painted on it as far as the elbow. I held it from me like a diseased member, and stumbled out into the clean afternoon light.

The water from the tap in the dairy was hard to get started. But when it came it felt like ice, bouncing off my skin and spraying my clothes. At the point where it struck, my arm showed a surprising white. I could feel myself shaking with rage as I watched the thruppenny bit flush to a gleaming yellow. *The embossed poker came down with savage force. The skull caved in like an eggshell.*

Turning off the stiff tap took a while and left me even wetter. I rubbed my arm until it hurt with the old towel hung inside the dairy door, then tossed it on the soaking floor. They hated when anybody did that, but there'd be no pictures after this anyway. To hell with the lot of them. Usually I made faces in the kitchen window as I pulled down the latch on the back door, but not tonight. Eyes straight ahead, I gripped the latch and pushed the door open with my knee.

The loaded box of eggs screeched as they pushed it across the kitchen floor. Anne and my mother were murmuring to each other but I didn't look up. Kicked off my wellingtons, gave the Sacred Heart a dirty look and marched upstairs. At every step I banged my foot as hard as possible, even though it hurt my heel. They thought they could make me walk quiet, do anything, but they were wrong. In my bedroom, the picture of Jesus with the thorns watched me as I changed my wet clothes. For a moment I thought about telling Him off, but decided not to.

My brown jersey with the hole and a pair of trousers with a button missing at the front were all I could find, but at least they were dry. I changed into them and was lying on the bed with *Adventures at Green Manor* when she barged in. Without knocking.

'What in the name of goodness kept you? Have you got the money?' She stood with her hands on her sides and her elbows sticking out.

'I have.'

'It took long enough. And what was all that noise on the stairs, pray tell?'

I put my face behind the book. 'Some of it fell in the groop and Daddy was giving out.'

She came closer, got a grip on my sleeve. 'Some what fell?'

'Some of the picture money. It just slipped.'

'The picture money!' She sounded like him now. Even looked like him, only her teeth were smaller and didn't come out.

'The groop was full and...I got it out again, though,' I said quickly. 'And washed it. Look.' I passed the thruppenny bit to her. She kept her hand out, so I poured the other coins into it as well.

'It was an accident. And then he started roaring, and...' I could feel the tears of self-pity pushing up again.

She let go of my sleeve and her voice softened. 'Well, there you are. Probably fate.' She nodded, as if remembering. 'Fate does some fierce things.'

I sat on the side of the bed and stared down at my feet. Big foot, small foot. 'One minute I was holding it. Then I looked up –'

'Here,' she said, rubbing the crispy hair at the back of my neck. 'Quit fretting. You're miles better off having a wee rest. Nobody's blaming you.' She checked the watch she'd got for selling a hundred books of Building Fund tickets. 'I'd better get going or I'll be late.'

The pattern of the linoleum under my feet became suddenly dangerous-looking. 'But – Daddy's raging. He was shouting like a bull.'

'Mm-m?'

'He'll never let us go now. Will he?'

'No. Mind you, I thought neither of us would get when I broke an egg doing the cleaning. Fate is funny sometimes.' She smiled and stood up. 'Still. You'll get again, to something miles better.'

I stared up at her. 'But – are you getting?'

'I didn't even ask! Here's me, cleaning the eggs, not saying a word. And next thing, he comes in and says, "You can go to the pictures, but let his lordship stay put."' She smiled kindly. 'Lep you into bed with your nice book. What is it anyway?' Unable to speak, I held it up. 'Oh, that. I started it one time – all house wings and codes of honour. Cheerio.'

She left, slamming the door behind her and clumping like a carthorse on the stairs.

I changed into my pyjamas and threw my jersey and trousers into the corner of the room as hard as I could. Knelt with my face buried in the eiderdown. Jesus had suffered for our sins, but at least there'd been no pictures then and He had no sister either. Through the open window came the crunch of gravel as Anne hurried out the lane. She was singing 'Goodnight, Irene' even though she didn't know the words. 'Laaa, Laaa, la-la, la-la. Laaa, Laaa, la-la.'

I champed on the bit of hard chewing gum I'd found stuck to the bottom of the Jesus picture. It took me a while to find my place.

Within minutes the flames had enveloped the stately pile. Jenkins, his face smudged, eyes wild, confronted Sir Jim. 'Oh sir!' he shouted. 'I heard screaming from the west wing – Lady Anna and the others must be trapped!'

Sir Jim cocked an ear, then shook his head. 'Can't hear a thing myself.' He passed a purse of sovereigns to the butler. 'See they get a good funeral, Jenkins.' Then, hands deep in his pockets, he crunched down the avenue towards a new life. The cattle in the fields watched him go, heard him whistling softly.

MUSIC AND ART

MISS MARTIN'S PIANO WAS LOVELY. It was a nice chocolate brown, not scratched and black like ours. All its keys worked and none of them had bits of their ivory missing. When I pressed them, it gave a rich cushioned sound. When Miss Martin pressed them, it made me think of stretching back in a warm bath. As she reached forward to turn a page the little brass clip on the stand for the music book winked in the evening light as if it knew a secret and would tell me later.

Miss Martin and her piano went well together. She had brown hair, and teeth that were crooked in a cheerful way. Her lips and wrists were plump, and she wore a gorgeous perfume that I could smell each time she moved. My lesson was on Friday evenings, and as I cranked through 'Bobby Shafto' she would tap time with her pencil on the wooden bit at the end of the keyboard, nodding her head and humming the tune. At the end she'd put her hand on my arm and say, 'Good boy, Jimmy. Now practise hard', even when I'd been rotten. I liked my lessons with Miss Martin.

And then, one evening in May, on my way home from a lesson, Bubbles McCann screeched 'Gee-ronimo!' and tried to jump on my back from the wall opposite the chapel. He

missed and landed, swearing, on the footpath. He was known
as Bubbles because he once hid in the hot press and watched
while his sister Eileen took a bubble bath. At least that's what
he said.

Hopping occasionally to rub his sore knee, he walked
down the Courthouse Hill alongside me. The cowboy picture in Miller's Picture House on Saturday had been the best
yet, he said. The baddy had got punched in the face five
times by Gene Autry, and when the girl had fallen backwards
over the dog you could see up into all her petticoats. Then
he noticed *Fifty Pianoforte Melodies* under my arm.

'What's that?' he said, tugging at them. Bubbles always
touched things when he could, as if to prove to himself that
they existed. In art lesson he nearly always did the best drawing, but Brother McGonigle would still end up roaring at
him because he had fingered the bowl of fruit or left a thumb
mark on a fresh painting.

I grabbed the music book back and told him Miss Martin
was teaching me the piano.

'Has she a cane?'

No, I told him, no cane. Just a pencil for tapping time. If
you hadn't practised during the week, she might sometimes
grab your hands and press them down on the right notes. But
no cane.

Bubbles leaned close to me, so I could smell the barley-
sugar on his breath. 'Our Eileen,' he whispered, 'would grab
the Pope. One day when I wasn't expecting it she grabbed
me through the lining of my trouser pocket. One minute I'm
reading Pudsy Ryan, next she's ripping bits off me.'

I gripped my music book tighter and tried not to blush.
When Miss Martin stood behind me, an arm on either side
of my shoulders, her perfume filled my head. Sometimes
when she leaned in to peer at a note, I could see up her

nostrils. They were always clean and without a single hair. When she leaned in to play over my shoulder, something warm and soft would rest on my back, then slither away as she sat back in her chair again.

When we drew level with Wee Mickey's shop, Bubbles stopped to stare at a paint set in the window. I walked on out the road home. I must have been nearly a hundred yards away when his shout came drifting after me: 'She's got a right pair on her, hasn't she?' I pretended not to hear.

Two days later, on Monday morning, Brother Pius McGonigle took a hanky from up his soutane sleeve and wiped his mouth with it. Then he got the pencils and paper from the press behind the blackboard and passed them out. He wanted us, he said, to draw a nature scene. A river, a mountain, maybe even just a field full of buttercups or thistles. Yes, there could be humans, but we mustn't forget Nature. Most important of all, though, we must see to it that every drawing was done from memory. The first man he got copying out of a book, he'd thump him till he saw stars.

I drew a fisherman by the side of a river. It looked all right. The fish on the end of the line came out a bit big, but it could be a salmon. Besides, the worms made up for it. They were in a tin on the grass, and I'd drawn it so you were look-ing down into the tin, could see the full brown wriggling ball. A few tiny touches of white on several of their backs to show they were shiny, then I turned to show it to Caruso Kelly in the desk beside me.

Caruso was gone. Or gone out of our seat. He was three seats up in the next row, leaning on the shoulders of Presumer Livingstone and Trigger Donnelly, peering in at Bubbles's drawing. Brother McGonigle had gone into the porch for a smoke, so I tiptoed up to look.

There were two drawings on Bubbles's desk. The first

showed a family picnicking in a field. Beside the spread-out tablecloth what looked like a mother and young boy were sitting. The boy's hands held the edge of the cloth and his expression was anxious. The woman had her hands in the air, fingers splayed in alarm. In a corner of the field a man, presumably the father, was being chased up a tree by a bull. It was well drawn but Caruso, Presumer and Trigger were concentrating on the second picture and grinning.

In this one the same three people – boy, woman, man – featured again. But there were a couple of big differences. Instead of a field, this drawing showed a room. The boy had the same startled expression, but now he was sitting at a piano, hands on the keyboard, and you could see beads of sweat bouncing from his forehead. The woman sat in a chair beside him and was bent forward about to grab his hands. Over her left shoulder there was a window, and through the window a tree was visible. A man was running towards the tree, followed by a bull. Over the man's head Bubbles had written 'Brother McGonigle', over the woman, 'Miss Martin', and above the boy, 'Guess Who'. The other major difference between this drawing and the first was even more striking. All three figures – boy, woman, man – were completely naked. All right, their backs were turned or their legs were in the way, so nothing really important showed, but they still hadn't a stitch on. My eyes kept going back to Miss Martin's left breast, which lay on her forearm like a baby seal. The other boys around Bubbles's desk were biting their hands and snorting with delight. Bubbles was smirking quietly and putting the finishing touches to one of the trees.

Who knows what I'd have done if at that moment the porch door hadn't opened and the Brother come back in? I might have murdered Bubbles and torn the drawing. Or maybe I'd have done nothing. Creating a scene would just let people know that I was a softy who made a fuss about drawing people with their clothes off. At the same time I felt a burning in my chest that Miss Martin should be treated in this way. That she should even be in Bubbles's mind with no clothes on seemed an attack on her. What right had he to take things out of his mind and draw them on a page, for people to snuffle at . . . But there was no time for that now. Brother McGonigle was standing at the door talking to someone, his back to us, and we slid quietly back into our desks. When I looked, Bubbles had slipped the second drawing out of sight.

That night I had a dream. Bubbles and I were alone in a white room with red furniture. Outside the window a herd of cattle was thundering past, making the floor shake like sitting on a tractor. I was seated on a stool with a dunce's hat on and Bubbles was standing at the window with his back to me. That made it easy for me to get off the stool and creep up on him. I had my father's saw in my hand, the one that went *whook! whook!* when you shook its blade. I grabbed Bubbles by the hair. 'Gee-ronimo!' I yelled, starting to saw at his neck. Soon there was blood everywhere – on the windowledge, on my arms – I even had to blink some of it out of my eyes. Luckily enough, what splashed on the furniture didn't show up because the furniture was red. Some blood did spill onto the floor but Bubbles, bleeding and smiling at the same time, bent down, gripped the floor and shook it like a bedsheet. The pools of blood bounced once, then drained down a mouse hole in the corner of the room. We nodded to each other and shook hands at the same time, like Laurel and Hardy, then sat down side by side to watch the sea of horns and dust stream past the window. No offence had been intended, I told Bubbles. It was just that I loved Miss Martin and would someday marry her, and part of picking somebody out to marry was that you protected their honour until the time came for her to be dishonourable with you. Bubbles nodded and laughed when I said that, and continued laughing even after his head had gone rolling along the floor. I could still hear chuckling from under the sofa as I woke up. My hairline, when I wiped it with my hand, was limp with sweat.

This couldn't go on. I had to get that drawing from Bubbles. One, it was Bubbles using the things I had told him about my music lesson to make a mockery of me and my teacher – a slimy, dirty sort of mockery. Two, looking at Miss Martin in the drawing gave me a warm glow like an electric fire, a glow that would be delicious to feel again. I closed my eyes. What had her back looked like? Had her bum flattened where it met the seat? I pulled the bedsheet around my mouth, breathed into it, made it warm. Someday Miss Martin would lose her key and have to come to my house to give me a piano lesson. My father and mother would be out when she rang the bell, and she'd follow me into the hall and say, 'I'm boiling, I need a bit of a bath before we do anything!' Then I'd show her the bathroom and she'd stop me going out again, would lean against the inside of the bathroom door the way women were always doing in the pictures. Then she'd ask me to be a good boy and loosen some buttons at the back of her blouse. Then it'd emerge that she had sprained her ankle the previous day and had been bravely hiding the fact. But now she could hide it no longer, because she needed help to get into the bath. So I'd help her. Once in, she'd put her head back, letting her hair spread out on the water like a fan, while the round parts of her in front floated glistening to the surface. She had her finger raised and crooked for me to come and soap her back when the bedroom door opened. My mother stared very hard at me and said if I lay a minute longer, my porridge would be stone cold.

At lunch time next day I hurried from the classroom and hid in the lavs. The cubicle didn't have a lock, but if you jammed your back against the door and propped your feet against the toilet bowl, nobody could get in. Not that anybody was trying – they were all out in the school yard, chasing each other with toffee-apple sticks or walking along the top of the yard wall with their eyes shut. Rigid against the lav door, I took a jam sandwich from my lumberjacket and started eating.

Supposing I just asked Bubbles for the drawing? Went up and said, Give us the picture, Bubbles. But then he'd say, What for? And even if I didn't tell him, he'd still make up something embarrassing and go and tell Caruso and Trigger and half the school. Hear what your man came to me looking for? Pisss wisss wisss wisss, dirty wee bugger. Unbearable, that would be. No, asking would be useless. The only way out was to steal it.

'Never take even a pin that's not yours,' my mother had always warned. But this wasn't a pin, this was a drawing of people with no clothes on. In a sense that my mother could never understand – *must* never understand – this drawing *was* mine. My words had created it for Bubbles. The piano, Miss Martin, my hands – practically everything. He had just stuck the nakedness on as an extra. Bubbles was only an instrument, the way a pen or pencil would be an instrument if you picked one up to write down your ideas. The boy's face might not look all that much like mine, but that didn't matter – it was still my drawing by rights. That was why I would be perfectly justified in going into the classroom, opening Bubbles's desk and taking it. By the time he discovered it was missing, I'd have it at home under my bed.

I trotted through the playground with my eyes down, in case some of the ones playing jailsies would ask me to join in. No one did. The wooden handle of the classroom door turned easily. Inside the room the sun shone through the window and caught chalk dust motes in its beam. The door made an echoing sound when I closed it.

Bubbles's desk was two rows across from mine at the back. He had left his pen stuck in the inkwell, a tiny triangle of blotting paper decorating its top like a flag. The desk lid, scored with generations of gouges and initials, creaked when lifted. Inside, a half apple lay in a corner, its cut side brown and dry-looking. I went carefully through the pile of disordered books. A sheet with a drawing of a dog, spittle hanging from its teeth, about to bite into a cat, the cat with its teeth parted to devour a mouse. Bubbles could really draw . . . I lifted an atlas; a fountain pen with a gold top slid from inside the spine of it. A week before the Christmas holidays, Brother McGonigle had got us all to pray to Saint Anthony to help find this pen. It meant more to him than any pen in the world, he said, because his mother had given it to him. But even though we prayed for a week and every desk had been searched, it could be got nowhere. Until now. As well as everything else, Bubbles was a thief.

Finally, at the very bottom, my drawing. A quick glance showed Miss Martin as even more lovely than I'd remembered her. And yes, where her bum met the seat it did flatten, just a little bit. The naked boy at the piano looked, if anything, less like me. I closed Bubbles's desk gently, wincing as it creaked again, and crossed to my own. Under *Junior Geometry* would be a good place to hide it. I had just lifted it and *Treasure Island* out of the way, and was taking a last peek at Miss Martin's feet – even they looked interesting – when the porch door opened and Brother McGonigle came in. He moved straight towards me, a trail of blue smoke from the cigarette in his left hand zigzagging behind him. Where it caught the shaft of sunlight it turned grey.

His voice was soft. 'What's this?' he said and took the drawing from my hand. 'Hmm?'

I tried to speak but a raw quarter-spud seemed to have got stuck in my throat. Instead, the hair on my neck crinkled and I stared hopelessly at the iron leg of a desk. The friction from hundreds of young boots had worn its bottom bit shiny.

Brother McGonigle's voice came from above me, slightly thick as if he needed to clear his throat. 'That's lovely,' he said slowly, and I heard the sound of tearing paper. Then more tearing, and more, the Brother now grunting with the effort. Finally a flutter of pieces into the wastebasket beside my desk. 'A lovely use of your God-given talent.'

I stood, eyes on the floor. This must be how a salmon felt when the gaff went in. I wanted to grab his sleeve, tell him that it had been Bubbles, not me – that I actually *disapproved* of the drawing, that was why I'd nyucked it. But I knew it'd be useless. Bubbles would deny everything, and the Brother would then add cowardice and lies to my original crime of impurity. I squeezed my eyes shut and spoke to God at a very quick speed. Listen, dear God, let us off this time and as long as I live, I'm serious, I will never look near a naked woman. On paper and everywhere else, I'm finished with them. Amen. Then I began to cry.

When some people cry, their noses don't run, it's their eyes. I'm the other way round. The first tear has hardly dribbled past my cheek when my nose starts, big wads of stuff coming down on strings, practically choking me when I try to sniff them back up. The top of the desk was splashed in tears too, some of them falling on my exercise book and smudging the sums.

I was still crying when Brother McGonigle called for the class to pay attention. They had filed in and were staring from me, huddled in my desk, gasping and sniffing, to him, straight and unblinking at the front. Piss wisss wisssss, they said. What's happening? Pisss wisss wisss.

'This,' said the Brother, gripping my shoulder, 'is Master James Rice. Look at him good and hard.' He paused while they looked. Then he pulled my jacket collar and raised me, like a dead chicken on a hook. 'For Master Rice is a corner boy AND a boy who spends his day drawing' – he made a face as if someone had let off – 'impurities.'

There was a gasp round the class. Boys who'd stolen lead off Protestant church roofs, boys who'd taken money from the Vincent de Paul box, boys who'd written bad words on bits of paper and stuck them down the front of wee girls' blouses – they all sat there sucking in their breath and shaking their heads. Bubbles too. I felt my indignation so strong it pushed back my fear a little bit. 'Spends his day drawing,' the Brother had said! Even it had been me did the drawing, I wouldn't have spent a day at it. I wanted to protest but didn't dare.

Brother McGonigle took a hanky from his sleeve, wiped his hands on it, stuffed the hanky out of sight again. 'Some of you are wondering – I have a sixth sense, that's how I know; it's in the air – some of you are wondering, What was in this drawing? What form did its impure contents take?' His eyes moved over the class like a searchlight. From a murmur, his voice went up to a roar: 'WHO CARES?' He let the words vibrate around the classroom, off the windows, the blackboard, the door to the porch. Only when they'd died did he speak quietly again: 'Offensive. Filthy. That's all you need to know.' His head lowered as if in prayer. 'Spittle in the face of Our Lady.'

Terror gripped me. Maybe I should tell him about his mother's pen being hid in Bubbles's desk? No. He'd probably label me an informer and come down twice as hard. Brother McGonigle was like that.

He talked a bit more about pure snow and buckets of tar. Then he reached inside his desk and produced The Major. This was a long leather strap, springy and flexible, that wobbled up and down in his grasp as if it was alive.

'Hand!' I inched my hand, small and curled, towards him. He glanced briefly towards the class. 'Let this be an example to all of you.'

Six zingers, with the weight of his shoulder behind them. Each time the strap came down, my knees buckled a little further, so by the last I was almost hunkered on the floor. Finished, he tossed the strap onto the desk, rammed his hands into his soutane pocket and walked down the aisle between the seats, whistling silently. He always did that when he was really really upset about something. Then: 'Treasure Islands, gentlemen', and everybody breathed relief, rummaged in their desks.

Hunched in my seat I sucked and blew on my fingers time about. They were white and numb at the tips and felt like they had been attached to the ends of my arms by mistake. Caruso, Bubbles and the others were watching me, I knew, but I didn't look up. I fumbled open my copy of *Treasure Island*. Squeezed my hands between my thighs while the Brother's voice rumbled somewhere in the distance. Waited for the world to put its splintered pieces together again.

That Friday, Miss Martin looked so beautiful I felt afraid: eyes shining, hair silky, perfume like a drug. If I held her gaze, all that I felt and the secrets about her that I had seen on a piece of paper would show in my face. So I stared instead at the piano keys and tried not to blush. I'd been doing 'Polly Put the Kettle On' and 'Three Blind Mice' for ages, but I still stumbled at least four times in each. My fingers seemed to have swollen even thicker and clumsier than usual; and where had the black rims of dirt edging all ten nails come from? It was as if they belonged to somebody else and that person wasn't on my side. With six minutes left, Miss Martin played through 'Over the Waves', my next piece for learning, to show me how it was done. She made it sound wistful and lovely. When I tried, I murdered it. In the end she gave a little cough and said it was nearly time, and by the way did I know a boy called Robert McCann. Mouth dry and tongue a cripple, I stammered I did.

Her bow-shaped eyebrows rose, her plump lips opened in a smile. Little bits of wet gleamed around her teeth. 'A strange wee boy, that! He landed at my door today with this.' She reached under her music case and produced a brown envelope. 'Said he'd done it at school and his mammy thought I might like it.'

I reached out for it and my right hand shook so much I had to grip it with my left. Once again he had drawn three people: a boy quite like Bubbles himself this time, only better-looking, hair parted, playing the piano; a woman very like Miss Martin, smiling slightly, bending to show him a note on the keyboard; and outside, through the window, a man with a net in his hand, chasing a butterfly through a field. All of them had their clothes on.

'Robert McCann,' she said again, pointing to the signature at the bottom, with the R for Robert and the M for McCann far too big. 'How he knows I have a piano even is beyond me. Though he has improved on the real article.' With a little laugh of pleasure, she leaned forward and put her hand on my arm. Her perfume tunnelled up my nose and into

the empty room of my brain. 'The artist's eye, I suppose . . .
What else has he drawn, this, ah, Robert?'

'Oh, windows and cows and things,' I said, and began to
play 'Over the Waves' quite quickly even though she hadn't
told me to. The notes were like stones hurled into the room.
Under my jersey, my chest was tight and my heart was
shivering like a whipped pup.

Saints and sinners

Nipper McGrath was not the religious type. He had thick hairy arms and squat hairy thighs (you notice things like that when you're sharing a room with someone) and when he was talking to you he would sometimes lean forward, grin and pinch you really viciously. Hence his name – Nipper. He also liked to tell anyone who would listen – usually me, after lights out – about experiences he had had with a friend of his sister's called Patricia in the back of his uncle's car. There were boys who stayed behind in the chapel after night prayers, kneeling upright among the shadows praying for God's guidance in their lives. But Nipper was not one of them.

So when, on the evening of 16 March 1957, I came on him standing at the back of the chapel, I was surprised. The next day was Saint Patrick's Day. Most boys had hurried off to collect shamrocks or discuss plans for our day out in town. Nipper however was positioned beside the statue of Saint Patrick, softly hissing 'Hail Glorious Saint Patrick' and rubbing the great man's toe. I looked away in the hope that I could get past without being spotted. Useless. He gripped my sleeve, drew me towards him. Nodding, he put an arm around my shoulder before taking in his fist some flesh on my upper back.

'Listen,' he said in his throaty growl. 'You're a good judge of women. What do you think of Biddy?'

Biddy was the best-looking of the six maids who brought us our meals from the kitchen. She had fair hair and muscles that rippled on the back of her bare legs when she pushed a trolley. I looked as enthusiastic as I could and said I thought Biddy was dynamite.

For a moment his grip slackened and he nodded at the mosaic tiles of the chapel floor. Then it tightened again. 'What would you say if Biddy wrote to you?'

I hesitated. Was he saying that Biddy actually had written to me – that he had a letter from her? Unlikely, but you never knew. I said I would be amazed to receive a communication from someone as gorgeous as Biddy.

'She wrote me a note this morning.' He smiled, reliving the event. 'I put my hand to the bottom of my porridge bowl and there it was, taped.'

'Did she address it to you? I mean, did it say, ah, Dear Nip –'

'No need for Dear Anythings. I already told you, it was taped to the bottom of my bowl. *My* bowl.'

I nodded hard, looked impressed. 'So what did it say?'

'"Meet me at Governor Walker's statue at half-one tomorrow. Love and kisses, Biddy."' Nipper smiled broadly between clenched teeth and at last let go. 'Love and kisses – you ever hear the like of that?' I said I hadn't. 'That's why I'm rubbing Stonearse here' – he nodded towards Saint Patrick, who went on staring straight ahead as if he hadn't heard. So many hands had rubbed Saint Patrick's toe it was shiny black, in contrast to the rest of him which was smoke grey, including the snake he was standing on. 'He's the boy will make sure she turns up and gets stuck in.'

The idea of praying to our national saint for a hot coort sounded a bit dangerous to me. Sacrilegious, in fact. But I smiled and nodded and said Saint Patrick had got many's a thing in his time. Hands deep in trouser pockets, we stood on the steps of Senior House. I kept a small smile on my face, in case he thought I wasn't enjoying his company.

There was about an hour of daylight left. The Dean, pale and talking away to himself, had pulled the four KEEP OFF THE GRASS signs from the college lawn and stacked them in a neat pile on the gravel. Now he was gesturing for boys to begin looking for shamrocks. 'Here – come on!' he shouted, grabbing two small boys by the blazer collar and thrusting them onto the grass. 'It'll be dark as a coal cellar if you don't shift.'

We watched him gesture and call, prodding boys into doing what he normally would have punished them for. Gradually the lawn filled, some boys kneeling, some crouched with their bums in the air, all searching for enough shamrocks to fill their buttonholes the next day. Upright, the Dean moved among them, a white face above a black soutane, smiling and occasionally having a quiet word with himself.

In bed that night we could hear the maids' radio in the kitchen below. It was tuned to Radio Luxembourg and playing 'Heartbreak Hotel'. Dishes clattered, instructions were shouted, someone laughed. Down there somewhere Biddy worked, maybe emptying a teapot or scraping cold porridge from a tin dish. Thinking of Nipper. Not knowing how hard he could nip.

From the bed by the window Nipper's voice came softly. 'Hi. Hear your man Elvis?' We listened together. 'Did you know he has only one arm?' In the darkness I shook my head. 'Left one – gone from the elbow. Has a plastic yoke under his sleeve for holding the guitar up.' There was a pause. 'Has to wear trousers with a zip.'

The following morning after the special mass, boys poured down the college walks. Their hair was larded with Brylcreem, their faces had been freshly shaved, each button-hole was a limp explosion of green. People who normally growled, smiled broadly. Clusters of boys moved togther, jostling each other onto the lawn in their hurry to get out.

I guessed that Nipper would try to attach himself to me, so after breakfast I hung around the senior classroom huts, peering into each in turn as if searching for a lost textbook. By the time I emerged, the walks had largely emptied. My coat over my arm, I moved briskly towards the gates. Before I reached them, though, I heard the thud of boots begin. Nipper, a grin on his face and blood oozing from two, no, three pimples on his chin, trotted alongside.

'Nearly missed you,' he said, producing a packet of Sweet Afton cigarettes from his trouser pocket. I tried not to think of where they'd been or that they seemed slightly warm. We lit one each and walked slowly along the top of the old city walls. Small groups of boys were already there, standing in clusters around Roaring Meg and other cannon from the siege talking excitedly and sometimes spitting over the wall. Few adults came this way, which made it a good place to smoke. Nipper and I kept on walking until we reached Governor Walker's statue at the end. We lit another Sweet Afton each and stood tapping our ash over the edge of the wall into the Bogside below.

Neither of us mentioned the fact that there was no sign of Biddy. Nipper said that he'd like to try to climb up and put a po on Governor Walker's head. 'Or a pair of knickers,' he added, 'in bad need of a wash.'

While I twitched and fidgeted, Nipper stood relaxed, his

backside against the wall, talking about people who had jumped from aeroplanes and lived. How would he react if she didn't come, I wondered. Would he sulk, rage, laugh? And what should I say? The wrong word could lead to terrible retribution.

Just as I thought I would have to make a run for it or start to scream, a figure appeared about a hundred yards along the wall. It wore short trousers and was running towards us. Closer, it proved to be a small boy with see-through snot on his upper lip. Pumping his elbows needlessly high, he ran past the other groups of smokers until he was ten yards from us, then stopped. 'Biddy says she can't come,' he yelled, 'but she'll meet you in the Rialto cinema at three o'clock!'

A cheer went up from some of the other groups, and there were a few shouted suggestions as to what Nipper could do with her when they got to the cinema. Swearing through clenched teeth, Nipper chased after the boy, who scrambled over the railings of the Protestant church behind him and into the graveyard. Nipper followed, dodging round the tombstones, and then over the railings at the other side and down Magazine Street. We could hear him shouting at the child to go home and blow his snotters into a sheet or something. There was a brief silence. Then Nipper appeared again, panting. 'That wee shite needs braining,' he said with a small smile.

We finished our cigarettes and moved on. Just walking beside Nipper made me feel uncomfortable, like being near a dog you know has fleas. And yet it wasn't until we were at the Rialto box office and the wee woman with the knitting was tearing off two back stall tickets and Nipper's hairy hand had pushed the money through the little glass hole to her, that my scruples began to bite. When we had a religious retreat at the college, at least one day was spent on sermons about impurity. There was a choice, the priest said. We could live like Irishmen or like Hollywood stars. We could have big cars and swimming pools or a conscience at peace with God. We could take an Irish road that led to happiness, or a Hollywood road that led to hell. But not both. It was up to us. And even if we said we weren't going to go down the Hollywood road but would associate with people who were getting ready for the Hollywood road, we were still in trouble. Because that was an occasion of sin, and an occasion of sin was a sin too. That was the thing about sexual pleasure – even coming within a six-mile radius of it could be fatal.

So where did that leave me now? By the time Nipper was through coorting Biddy at the pictures his soul would be as black as coal. That meant if my soul rubbed up against his – if I aided and abetted him by going in there with him – then I would be ripe for damnation as well. It was a terrifying thought. Say a bus hit me coming out of the pictures? I'd be sent cartwheeling into the flames of hell for Nipper McGrath, someone I didn't even like.

As we got settled into our seats Gene Kelly, Donald O'Connor and Debbie Reynolds had started to jump over the back of a couch, singing as they jumped. How marvellous to have a chum like Debbie Reynolds. Or even Gene Kelly or Donald O'Connor. Beside me, Nipper was sucking between his teeth and peering around in the gloom.

'Listen!' he whispered. 'In front of the geezer with the baldy head – is that her?' It wasn't.

It was difficult watching a film with Nipper. Debbie had begun to show little bits of her legs when she danced, which was nice and at the same time friendly. But each time someone came in, Nipper grunted and corkscrewed his head round to see them. And even when he was watching the film, he wouldn't keep quiet. 'Look – see that? Trick photography. Your man Kelly can't dance. Barely walk, even. Hurt his back in a picture two years ago trying to lift Jane Russell.' He reached into his pocket and took out two bars of Crunchie. Thrust one of them into my hand, unwrapped the other and began to eat noisily.

The green clock to the left of the screen showed quarter to four. Smoke twisted up from the seats occupied by college boys and was speared on the light from the projector. Scattered throughout the cinema there were maybe a dozen adults, lonely individuals chewing sweets and, like Nipper, glancing round every time someone came in.

When the singin'-in-the-rain scene ended, Nipper elbowed me. 'Keep my seat. She could be in the gallery.' He crushed the Crunchie paper in one hairy hand and threw it towards the screen, then vanished into the dark, humming 'Hail Glorious Saint Patrick'. I could have told him that the gallery was shut – they always lock it during matinée performances in case a youngster goes in and falls over the edge. But I let him go. God obviously had created this opportunity especially for me. He'd taken Nipper away and left me a chance to slip clear of the net of sin.

At a price, that is. What had to be done would mean missing what happened to Debbie Reynolds, who I'd started to love for her personality as well as her legs. But better doing without Debbie than risk being roasted in the same corner of hell as Nipper. Swiftly, quietly, I entered the toilets in the foyer, inserted a penny and locked the cubicle door behind me. In here I'd be all right with God. Nipper could look after himself.

Have you ever spent three quarters of an hour in a toilet? Somebody had ripped the seat off and taken it away, and the air was heavy with the smell of tin buckets and Dettol. The first thing I did was take my hanky and rub it carefully along the rim of the bowl. Afterwards I put it back in my pocket and promised myself I'd send it to the laundry next Tuesday night. I then eased myself onto the bowl in a hunched-forward position, so my behind didn't slump into the depths.

With closed eyes, I concentrated for the first fifteen minutes on remembering the girl with black hair I'd seen at a *céilí* at Christmas. I hadn't danced with her or even spoken to her, but that wasn't how it was now. I was still ten yards from her when she ran towards me, smiling, and wrapped her arms round me. The *céilí* music changed to a slow waltz by Tennessee Ernie Ford, and her hair smelt like a lemon against my cheek. We took a long walk to the Lovers' Retreat outside the town on a summer evening, and we went to the pictures together, and finally on a holiday in Spain with me driving a brand-new car. She wore the same frock to all three places, a white one with lacy bits around the hem. Any jokes I told her she laughed at, with her head back and her mouth open. At one point she reached across a Spanish restaurant table and rubbed my arm. It wasn't an occasion of sin because it was meant as pure friendship.

After that I took out my comb and did my hair twice, wiping the Brylcreem from the comb's teeth with a bit of toilet paper. Then I cleaned my nails with a match, counted to one hundred ten times, and held my breath to a count of fifty. Very faintly I could hear the music and talking of the picture. At one point it sounded like Debbie Reynolds crying, and, later on, her laughing. Could I last another half-hour of this? I was wondering if hell could be much worse when I heard the outside door to the toilets open.

Solid footsteps – adult feet – clicked along the marble floor. Almost immediately I knew with complete certainty, don't ask me how, that he would come into the cubicle next to mine. And he did. I heard the coin being pushed in, the door opened, locked again from the inside. There was some heavy breathing, the twang of braces, a long sigh.

It's awful sitting in a toilet cubicle next to somebody. To do with sound and smell. And the things you start picturing the person next door doing to match their sounds. But this time it was worse still, because I had developed a very strong idea about the identity of the person on the other side. Afraid to swallow now, I lifted my elbows from my knees, a rigid, terrified statue. And as I did so, the person next door began to chuckle and talk.

There were several possibilities to explain this. It could be that two people had entered the toilets in perfect step, walked across to the next cubicle as one man, and entered it. And were now talking. Or I could be hallucinating. Unlikely though, either of these possibilities. Far more likely then that the Dean was at this moment within three feet of me.

Had he seen me? No, impossible. He'd have had to lie full length with his cheek against the marble floor to see even my ankles. And the Dean wasn't going to get his good suit ruined for the likes of me. Then a question swam into view: had Nipper located Biddy yet? Because if he had and the Dean came on the two of them, Nipper would be expelled. That was a rock-solid certainty. The Dean could be surprisingly relaxed about certain things – unmade beds, unpolished shoes, even talking in the chapel. But he was death on sexual pleasure.

'No need to mention it,' the voice next door said, giving a little chuckle. My heart lurched and jumped like a pup in a bag in a river. My elbow against the door to minimise the noise, I eased back the bolt of my cubicle. Started to tiptoe across the floor. My breath was coming in little gasps – would he be able to recognise me from them? Probably not. I pulled open the door leading into the foyer and behind me, the sound of humming coming from the toilet. It sounded a bit like 'Hail Glorious Saint Patrick' but I didn't stop to check. The door closed quietly and I trotted across the carpeted foyer.

Inside the auditorium again it was dark, the music and voices from the screen booming, the laughter from the audience puzzling. I didn't know where to start looking for Nipper and Biddy. They could be anywhere. Ears burning, I dug my nails into the palms of my hands. Where would I go if I had...? Of course, the back seat. I should have known that. Especially the double seats with no armrest. If I were intent on sin, that's where I'd go. And where Nipper would go, if he'd met her.

It was Biddy I spotted first – her fair hair stood out in the gloom. She was in the back row at the far side from where I'd started searching. Her face was completely turned away towards the back and she was kissing and being kissed by her partner in sin in a slow, Hollywood way. Half-trotting, ignoring the sighs and occasional protest as I came between people and the screen, I pushed along the second row from the back until I was opposite them. 'Here, Nipper!' I said, tugging at his sleeve. 'Nipper, for God's sake!'

Biddy's head pulled back and she stared at me. Her eyes looked sleepy and her mouth hung open, like a child that doesn't understand. I was thinking that I'd never seen her looking nicer when I noticed her partner's face. The lipstick on one cheek looked odd; but more important, it was not the face of Nipper. Below a Tony Curtis hairstyle and above a string tie, two brandy-ball eyes I'd never seen before stared out.

'Supposing I nip you instead,' their owner said in a voice like sandpaper. 'Stick your face up your arse for to give you a view.'

Apologising, I backed away. By the time I found Nipper I could feel my ears burning out of control. He was sitting on his own halfway down, flicking used tub lids at a group of boys six rows in front.

'Where'd you get to?'

'The bog,' I said. 'Do you know who's here? The Dean. He –'

'I saw him,' said Nipper, sending another lid slicing six rows forward, where it hit a small boy in the neck. 'Bugger came in and sat in that seat behind me for a full ten minutes. Had to put my foot on a whole fag. Bugger.' He flicked another lid, this time missing. 'Where'd you see him?'

I explained about the laughing and talking in the lavatory cubicle. 'But listen. Somebody else is here too.'

'Who?'

I hesitated for a moment. Maybe I shouldn't mention it. After all, there was no need to. Not now.

'Who?' His voice was harder.

'Not sure. But I think I saw... Biddy. Over there.'

Nipper sat up straight in his seat, looking suddenly serious. 'Where? What are you talking about?'

'Biddy is over the far side.' I took an extra breath. 'Getting stuck into a guy with a Tony Curtis hairstyle.'

Nipper raised his eyebrows, then sat back and smiled between his teeth. 'Well. Free country, I suppose.'

I stared. 'But you were supposed to meet her! And now she's, she's over there and –'

'Come round and sit down.' Nervous, I did so. He leaned forward and patted my shoulder. 'Keep a secret?' I nodded, wishing I didn't have to. 'Remember what I said about meeting Biddy? A yarn, the whole thing. A cod.' He held his hands slightly in the air, palms facing towards me, like a man surrendering. 'Just a laugh.' He pointed at the screen. 'See your man O'Connor – the one dancing on the plank? He was a monk for years before he got into the pictures.'

'But the wee fellah with the snotty nose said Biddy was going to meet you!'

Nipper took a quick glance to either side. 'Gave him sixpence to do it. Good actor, isn't he?' He leaned his head close to mine until I could smell the sweets and cigarette smoke. A grip like a fire fastened on the flesh between my elbow and shoulder. 'And you'll not tell anyone, sure you won't? Because, you do and I'll beat you good-looking. Comprenez, mon cheri?' He rummaged in his blazer pocket. 'Here, have a Malteser. I got a bag of them.'

And he propped his feet up on the back of the seat in front of him and dropped three Maltesers into his mouth. Cheeks bulging, relaxed. Between that and the end of the film a half-hour later we smoked three Sweet Afton each. Twice we checked to make sure the Dean was gone. Or rather, I did. My route was to walk cautiously along the empty bit at the back, looking along each row from behind. No Dean. Just boys slouched in their seats, looking a bit tired and even bored. Some of the adults who were sitting alone had fallen asleep.

By the time Gene Kelly had got his arms around Debbie Reynolds at the end and kissed her mouth and the whole orchestra had soared and the curtain come down, my teeth were clogged with chocolate, my tongue swollen from smoking, and my shirt was clinging to my back. But I felt good. Relieved, really. If a bus hit me now when I went outside, it'd be all right – I was free from sin. And so was Nipper – mortal sin anyway. The daft thing was that he was free from mortal sin because he'd told a pack of lies. As for Biddy and the Tony Curtis guy – well, they'd be well advised to look left, right and left again before crossing the road. The lipstick on his cheek, the look on her face . . .

As the seats thudded upright and we filed towards the glare of daylight the strains of 'Singin' in the Rain' filled the picture house. I checked my green buttonhole, which had begun to go a bit grey. Really, when you listened to it, 'Singing in the Rain' was practically the same tune as 'Hail Glorious Saint Patrick'. Only where Saint Patrick plodded along, the pictures music leapt and danced.

QUESTIONS AND ANSWERS

EDDIE QUINN STOOD LOOKING DOWN AT US, his lower lip wet, his chest heaving up and down as if he were going to have another of his fits. From where we were lying you might have thought he was laughing, but that was just the angle – us on the ground, him standing over us – and the way his mouth hung open as he panted. In fact he was waiting for us to respond to the sensational news he had brought.

He had come direct from the empty French classroom in Senior House, he said, where he had been squinting through a 2s. 10d. pocket telescope. He'd been trying to get a good look into the house across the street, where everybody knew a prostitute lived because you'd see a light on there at the oddest hours of the day and night. Tucker Deans had once hidden behind the handball alley and watched until midnight to see if he could see any action. Not a thing. The prostitute must have spotted him and lain low. But anyway, there was Eddie peering through the telescope, only when he did, a bit of fluff obscured his vision. So he was rubbing his eye and thinking about taking the telescope apart, when a piece of paper lying in the grate caught the eye he wasn't rubbing. The paper was burnt black but you could still read the writing. 'Latin,' it said. '5A and 5B. Answer all questions.'

Now, if he'd wanted, Eddie could have left us stretched in the long grass, smoking and talking about football and girls we said we'd gone up lanes with during the summer but never had. He could have found out all about the Latin paper himself, gone into the exam the next day and got the highest mark in the class. If it had been me, that's what I'd probably have done. But Eddie's mind works differently from mine or yours. He ran straight to us. And now here he was, chest going up and down, waiting for us to react.

Whistles of amazement, swearwords whispered again and again. Nicking our cigarettes, we scrambled to our feet.

'Are you sure it was the Latin paper?' Billy McKinney asked.

Eddie nodded. 'Mind you, I only saw the top bit.' He took off his wire glasses and began polishing them with a greyish handkerchief. Unprotected, his eyes looked small and pink.

'God Al–bucking–mighty,' Snots Casey said. 'What good's the top bit? You're not going to pass the exam from just knowing the top bit. God Al–bucking–mighty.'

Snots had hated Eddie since third year. It had been a wet Saturday afternoon and some people were arguing about where Floyd Patterson was from. Snots had insisted it was Africa and Tucker Deans had said no, it was Louisville in America. And then just when people had begun to talk about Lamumba Bumba and pretended to beat jungle drums, Eddie had leaned in and whispered loudly to Snots that he had a lump of green snot sticking out of his right nostril. Eddie was trying to be helpful, but Snots nearly went mad. Hated Eddie from then on.

'Most of it was hidden,' Eddie said, pushing his glasses back on his thick nose and looking embarrassed.

'Squeezed up in a ball in the grate . . .'

Billy McKinney took a handball from his trouser pocket and sent it whacking against the alley wall. 'So the paper's still in the grate?'

Eddie nodded.

'If somebody hasn't lifted it by now,' Snots muttered.

Billy pocketed the ball and twisted Snots's ear quite hard. 'Snots,' he told him. 'Shut your arse.'

At a brisk pace we all headed for the French classroom.

The exam paper was still there. In the grate, half-crumpled, corners curled delicately, the handwriting black against the paper's ash-grey. You had to hold on to the mantelpiece with one hand and twist your head round to read it. 'Latin, 5A and 5B. Answer all questions.' To make out the next bit your nose had to be practically touching the grate. 'Translate into English the following passage.' But after that nothing, no matter how much you twisted your neck. Maybe an O, maybe an F, but it was impossible to tell.

'Pull her out a bit,' Billy McKinney said.

Eddie gripped his arm. '*Mind*, Billy. If you touch it, the whole works'll come apart.' His eyes squeezed shut behind bottle lenses. Thinking.

'Train a bat,' Snots said. 'Get it to hang upside down and read it out to you.' He gave a snorting laugh and went back to staring out the window.

'Yes!' – Eddie pointed at Snots's back – 'that's it! If we lifted someone up and put him in the fireplace, head first, so he's upside down and could call out what's written there. We could have somebody else writing it all down. Brilliant, Snots!' Eddie beamed and pounded Snots on the back. Snots looked as if he'd swallowed a piece of poo.

It took us just five seconds to decide that Mousey Devine should be the one lifted in to do the reading, because he was smaller and lighter than the rest of us. Mousey agreed, although he looked worried as he buttoned his blazer. For a minute we held him horizontal, so he could get used to it and we could get a feel for the weight of him. Then, like a sweep's brush, only a lot slower and gentler, we inserted him into the fireplace. Eddie crouched at a desk, pen poised to take the dictation. Snots followed Billy's instructions and took copies of *Lettres de mon moulin* from the glass cupboard. Slowly, showing he didn't like doing it, he placed them on desks around the room. It had been decided that if somebody came in, we would say we were revising French together.

Which was just as well. Mousey had got as far as the fifth word on the second line and Billy was wondering aloud what Mousey would do if we dropped a lit cigarette butt up the leg of his trousers and Mousey had tensed and started to swear and we were all shaking with laughter, when heavy footsteps sounded in the corridor outside. The Dean's? Immediately the four of us dropped Mousey, hurled ourselves into the desks, and began frantically reading *Lettres de mon moulin*. You could hear our panting all round the room. The footsteps drew level with our door, paused for a second . . . then passed by. The silence that followed was broken by moaning from Mousey, who lay half in, half out of the fireplace's brass surround.

'There's a bone broke in my neck, true as God,' he gasped, crawling into a desk. 'You stupid hoors.'

We tried everything: cajoled him, promised to look after him, offered money (3d. each), but it was useless. Mousey refused to be lifted again. No more lifting him. For a moment we were desperate. Then Eddie said all right, use him. We looked at each other. Eddie would be harder to get a grip of and a lot heavier than Mousey, but on the other hand we would know what he was saying. Mousey's words tended to run into each other when he got excited. So even though we knew our strength would be pushed to the limit, we said yes.

'O FONS BANDUSIAE,' Eddie called in a clear whisper, holding his glasses in place and spelling as he went. 'S-P-L-E-N-D-I-D-I-O-R V-I-T-R-O.'

This was much better. Inside two minutes Snots had a full poem transcribed.

'Right, let us up, let us up quick,' Eddie called, beginning to cough.

We staggered back and manoeuvred him onto his feet again. He stood gulping, the blood flowing slowly back from his face, down his neck and into his body again. Then he had to sit for a minute on the edge of a desk. 'It's no joke being upside down.'

'Except when it's me,' Mousey said sullenly.

Billy tried to grab him round the neck but Mousey jumped clear, swearing.

Slowly, very slowly, Eddie slid one of the *Lettres de mon moulin* underneath the burnt exam paper and carried it to the windowsill. Using a comb and pencil, he eased back the curled corners. Fifteen minutes of peering and checking later, we had deciphered three more sentences, two irregular verbs and most of a paragraph from Caesar's *Gallic War: Book I*. It was only when Eddie tried to unwrinkle the last half-page that the comb slipped, a huge hole appeared and tiny curraghs of ash floated behind the radiator.

'Brilliant,' Snots said. 'Now we'll get everything in the first half of the paper right and everything in the second half bucking wrong. Frigging brilliant.'

'You know, Snots,' Billy McKinney said gently, 'you'd probably look better with no teeth.' He was going to make Snots promise to write deliberately wrong answers for every single question in the exam, but we persuaded him Snots wasn't worth it.

The exam hall was really the gym and the gym was really four adjoining classrooms with their partitions pulled back. The desks were lined up in straight rows the whole way from the back to the front to make it easier for the teachers supervising to catch you using cogs. Some teachers spent the exam at the front, reading the newspaper, but others spent the whole time tiptoeing around. There was always a smell of sweat in the hall.

The floor by the right-hand door had a stain, turned brown now, where Joe McMonagle's nose had once pumped blood. The PE master had thrown a medicine ball before Joe was ready for it.

But this wasn't a game. Pens scratched on sheets of foolscap. Fingers snapped to ask for more paper. Coughs and sighs floated up the ropes, climbed frames and echoed in the ceiling. Hands deep in his soutane pockets, Big Mick Maguire moved up and down, making no noise even on the bits of the floor that creaked. Joe McMonagle claimed Mick had lost both legs in an accident and that under the soutane were just two metal posts with castors on the ends of them. If it wasn't for the way Mick breathed through his long straight nose, you'd never have known where he was. Even when he was standing still, his nose whistled and rasped. Breathe in, whistle, breathe out, rasp. When he stopped and stared over your shoulder at what you were writing he would stop breathing completely for a minute; then he'd move on, whistling and rasping harder than ever.

The clock under the crucifix at the front said two o'clock – another half-hour to go. I'd been awake until midnight the night before, under the bedclothes with a torch, going through the known part of the paper with a Latin–English dictionary and an English–Latin dictionary. It was so stuffy I could hardly breathe, and my eyes kept getting filled with dust, but now I knew it had been worth it. Snots had been right: the second part of the paper was a stinker. Twenty lines of Latin poetry written by some madman. 'Arma virumque cano.' 'I am singing with the arm and the man.' Or was it 'To the arm and the man'? Neither made sense.

Eddie's behind bulged over the seat edge in front of me. I checked that Mick was far away, then reached forward my foot. No response. I prodded him again. Still nothing. 'Eddie!' I said, talking like a ventriloquist. 'What's the first line of the trans mean?'

It was like something that happens in a dream, only in a dream you can run away. Instead of answering, Eddie groaned and let the top half of his body topple from the desk. Really topple. He didn't stop until his left cheek pressed against the scuffed floorboards. After that there was complete silence in the hall for about two seconds. Only Eddie's breathing could be heard, like a cow going to have a calf. Then Big Mick came charging the length of the hall, soutane billowing.

'What is this pupil doing out of his desk?' Mick's bulging eyes stared at me, willing an answer. But it was Mousey, in the desk across from Eddie, who spoke.

'Took a fit, Father. Quinn's always taking fits.'

In the aisle Eddie lay twisted awkwardly, his legs caught under the desk, a string of whitish spittle hanging from his mouth.

'No one spoke to me of this. Seizures, you say?' Snots nodded. Big Mick wiped his own lips with a handkerchief, then his forehead as well. 'Right. In which case, four men – you, you, you and you – take a grip on his legs and middle. *Easy*! . . . I've got his head and trunk.'

Mousey was almost dancing with excitement. 'Father, where people take fits, you know, seizures and that, if you shift them, you can kill them. Their head needs blood, and lying on the floor gives it to them. I'm telling you. It was in the *Reader's Digest*.'

'Devine, as God is my witness...' Big Mick spoke between his teeth as he gathered Eddie under the armpits and nodded to indicate we all should lift. For the second time in twenty-four hours I found myself holding one of Eddie's legs.

Mousey ran ahead of us opening doors, peering back at Eddie's lolling head and muttering that we'd be sorry for shifting him. By the time we got to the infirmary Matron had the starched white sheets folded back. Still moaning, Eddie was laid on top of it. Matron felt his forehead, then pulled back the lids of his eyes. Eddie looked as if he had died, with so much white showing and the eyeball just hanging there in the middle. She wiped his mouth with a towel and said it was all right, the only problem was if he went to swallow his tongue, but the danger seemed to have passed.

'Thanks be to God,' said Mick.

Then Matron took a blanket from another bed and put it over Eddie, tucking the edge gently around his neck. There was something nice about the way she did that. He was still dribbling and making wheezing sounds. We wanted to stay in case Eddie might swallow his tongue, but Mick shooshed us out. 'Done a first-class job, lads – perhaps, who knows? helped save a classmate's life. Well done. Now I think it's time to leave him in Matron's good hands.'

'Will I tell you what's happening this minute?' Billy McKinney said, nudging me as we made our way downstairs again. 'Matron's good hands are taking the trousers off him. She's got a pair of stripy pyjamas all ironed, straight from the hot press, at the side of the bed. And when she has him bare-bum naked, she'll lift him, a leg at a time, and slide him into them. If he recovers halfway, he'll have a definite heart attack.'

Back in the hall some people were whispering, others writing furiously. Big Mick stood at the front and rapped a wooden duster on the table.

'You men,' he said. 'Because of the illness suffered by your classmate Edward Quinn, normal supervision has been breached. As you can see. For that reason, I want all of you now to take your pen and draw a line through whatever answers you have written to date. That's it . . . Yes, a straight line, diagonally drawn.' He demonstrated in the air. 'Through *all work*, yes, that is what I said, that is correct.'

There was a sort of collective gasp went round the hall. Several dozen pairs of eyebrows rose, hurt looks were exchanged. Was Mick suggesting that when he went out, we had attempted to . . . ?

'There is no slur intended on any boy. However, the opportunity to confer has been clearly available. For that reason – for that *reason*,' Mick said in a louder voice, above the buzz, 'this examination has lost its validity. Accordingly – ACCORDINGLY – your summer Latin mark will be calculated, not by examination performance here this morning, but by teacher estimation of your homework. Now. When I give the word, each row will bring up their answer sheets and place them in this wastepaper basket. Casey, sit quiet, young man, or I will warm your paws. The row along the wall first, please.'

After supper that night we all went to the sick room to visit Eddie. He was sitting up in bed finishing off a bowl of apple tart and custard. Billy took the chair by his bed. The rest of us stood around.

'All right now, Eddie?'

Before he could answer, Snots spoke. 'All right? With apple tart coming out his ears? Out his arse? Huh! *He's* all right.'

Eddie licked the spoon carefully and put the empty bowl on top of his locker. 'I heard about the Latin exam.' He shook his head. 'Terrible.'

Snots swung round from the window. 'What do you care? You got good marks for your homework, you bugger.' He turned to us, pointing to Eddie in the bed. 'Everybody keeps asking how he is. What about us? We're the ones that's been led up the garden-bucking-path.'

Mousey tapped Eddie's foot through the bedclothes. 'You had streels of white spit coming out your gob. I was sure you'd croaked it.'

'I was unconscious,' Eddie said, half-apologetically.

Billy stood, reaching into his pocket. 'Anyway it's nobody's fault if it didn't work. We all did our best.' He glanced in Snots's direction. 'And Eddie here went to loads of bother – told us about it, and let us lift him into the grate, and so on.' He stared at Mousey. 'Unlike some.'

'I did my best till yous tried to kill me,' Mousey said quickly.

Billy ignored him, turned back to Eddie. 'You need anything? Biscuits, maybe?'

'Every night at nine o'clock she brings us in tea and biscuits. But thanks, Billy. Honest.' Eddie fiddled with the sheets, eyes down. He seemed genuinely moved.

Billy nodded while we thought about Matron elbowing open the sickroom door to enter with hot tea and biscuits in the early summer dusk. Did she pour the tea? Did she sit on the bed and have a cup herself? The thought made the harsher, more active life beyond the sickroom door seem even less attractive than usual. Then Billy cleared his throat. 'Well, anyway, we think we should show we're grateful. About the exam paper and that. So if we each give you a bob for a, you know, get-well present, that'd even things up a bit. Right, boys?'

We shuffled, feeling embarrassed, reached in our trouser pockets. This was the first time Billy had mentioned it, but it seemed a fair enough thing, we all thought. Except, that is, for Snots.

'Get-well present? He is well! You saw him yourself, shovelling the dinner into him. Christ Almighty!'

'I've only ninepence,' Mousey said, putting the change on the bed.

Eddie struggled, tried to push the money back towards us. 'Snots is right – there's no need. And it didn't even help one of you.'

'Take it,' said Billy firmly. 'Us lifting you into the fire done it, I'd say. Brought on that oul' attack.'

Mousey rubbed his neck uneasily. 'You'd have to, you know, have a fit disease, before being held upside down like that would affect you.' He looked round, appealing. 'Isn't that right?'

Snots could hardly speak. 'He failed you in Latin, so you want to give him money! Give him a kicking, you mean.'

Billy put a hand gently on Snots's shoulder. 'Really, Snot? Where – in the arse? Is that the best place?'

'Listen, listen,' Eddie said. 'It's OK, Billy. Thing is, while I was sleeping –'

Billy tapped Snots on the chest. 'A shilling, shite-face. Or I'll grease my toe in your hole.'

Snots glared for a minute, then produced a shilling and threw it towards Eddie. It struck the wall above his bed, leaving a nick of white in the green paint. 'I hope you're in the lav when your next fit comes. And that you can't get the door open. And that you die pissing your trousers.' He slouched from the room, palming back tears of rage. As he passed me I put out my arm, but he jumped aside as if I was an electric shock.

Eddie watched Snots leave and shook his head sadly. Then sighed, lifted our money and piled it neatly on the top of his bedside locker. 'See when I was coming round from the turn? I heard voices. Knew it was Mick and Alfie even without opening my eyes.' He pointed to the door. 'They were over there.'

Mick and Alfie both taught history.

'What were they talking about?' said Billy.

'History!' Eddie said, his face bright with pleasure. He pulled a crumpled sheet of paper from inside his pyjama top. 'Number one, the Corn Laws, number two, Catholic Emancipation, number three, the rise of Parnell. I scribbled down everything I could remember once they left.'

Billy snapped his fingers. 'Irish history!' He liked Irish history – especially the rebellions. 'Right, then. Mousey, keep nix. Eddie, read it out. Jimmy,' he said to me, 'write it down so people can read it. All clear? And if anybody comes, hide the bloody thing. Right, Eddie – shoot.'

I took a used envelope from my jacket pocket and began to write carefully and neatly on its back. Mousey kept bobbing in and out the sickroom door. Eddie lay back in the bed, looking at the ceiling with a small smile on his face. And as I wrote, and the back of the envelope began to fill with information, I got this funny feeling. For the next few minutes – with Mousey fidgeting at the door, Billy standing at the window rattling coins in his pockets, Eddie dictating in his soft voice – for the next few minutes I felt really, really happy. It wasn't being rid of Snots – he'd be back the next morning girning twice as bad. And it wasn't feeling good for having given Eddie the bob either. In a way it was just being there, in that quiet room where Matron brought biscuits at nine every night and the world of bells and chalk and refectory was a distant echo. Like a golden syrup, happiness oozed up inside me, starting in my stomach, moving through my chest, filling my arms, my neck, my brain. Later, I knew, it would drain away, and I'd feel scrappy and dissatisfied again. But right now I was sixteen, full of the stuff of life, and about to get Irish history under control.

BOOING THE BISHOP

THE BISHOP LIVED IN A BIG HOUSE across the wall from our boarding school. On slow summer evenings we'd peep over and watch him playing croquet by himself, sometimes muttering and hammering the mallet into the ground when he missed a hoop. The grass on his side was as neat as a bebop haircut, and his shiny black shoes moved over it in tidy steps that never picked up any dirt. When his tea was ready, the housekeeper would stand outside the front door and ring a small handbell. Even if he had the mallet drawn back between his legs, poised to hit, he would drop it immediately and move at a smart pace to the house. Tweetie Downey claimed that on Sundays during the summer term the Bishop had a bowl of beans for tea. Then when we were in study hall, he would come out and zoom round the hoops like a balloon losing its air.

On Saint Patrick's Day every year he visited our boarding school. If he'd wanted, he could have opened a small door in the wall and simply walked through to us. Instead he entered through the front gates, a plump little figure half-lost in the back of a chauffeured Bentley. Among cushions he'd sit, smiling out at us with his little baby teeth, one white hand in midair sending blessings through the car's closed windows.

With a March breeze whipping our Brylcreemed hair, we would line the sloping driveway to clap and cheer as his car crunched slowly past. Behind us, knees bent and head low, the Dean trotted up the line abreast with the car. 'Now boys – clap! Quick, quick before he's gone past on you.' And if he thought we weren't enthusiastic enough, he'd prod the backs of the nearest boys and hiss, 'Applause! Applause!'

Then, on Saint Patrick's Day, 1958, somebody booed. Nobody could tell where it began. When we looked up and down the line everybody seemed to be still clapping, everybody's mouth was still open apparently cheering. But there was a boo. A travelling boo that started somewhere near the entrance gates and moved like a gnat-cloud up the line in time with the Bishop's car. You felt rather than heard it pass over you. To this day I don't even know if I booed myself.

Mercifully, sealed in the back of his car, the Bishop couldn't hear a thing. All through the heresy he went on smiling and blessing us. But the Dean heard it. There could be absolutely no doubt about that. The problem was, stumbling along, he couldn't tell *who* was doing it. If the Bishop hadn't been around, the Dean'd have waded in with strap flailing and made it his business to find out. But then if the Bishop hadn't been around, there'd have been no booing. So the Dean, poor man, went staggering up the line, his little groans of frustration mixing in with the boos and the clapping.

The car eased to a stop in front of the school and the Bishop was led into the chapel by the bowing and scraping sacristan. Once he was out of sight we broke ranks and hurried down the marble corridor, elbowing each other aside to get a fingertip in the holy water font. The air in the chapel was heavy with the smell of flowers and the altar cloth had a green edging. On the right-hand side a big chair with a

purple cushion was waiting for the Bishop's behind, and you
could see a trail of incense smoke coming out of the sacristy
door. For five, seven, ten minutes we sat coughing, whispering, waiting. When the mass was over we were all to get out
in the town for the rest of the day.

Then the organ in the gallery was thundering and the
Dean had led a line of altar boys out of the sacristy. Behind
them came the Bishop in his pointed hat and staff. He had
so much stuff on, it looked as if he might any minute vanish
inside the white and gold and purple. When the head prefect
in the front seat stood, so did we, hobnails clattering. We
bawled out the first lines of 'Hail Glorious Saint Patrick':

> Hail Glorious Saint Patrick, dear Saint of our isle,
> On us thy poor children, bestow a sweet smile,
> And now thou art high in thy mansion above
> On Erin's green valley look down in thy love.

Masses like this, with singing, were slower. Everything
stopped for the choir to perform the different hymns and
things in Latin. Stopped again when the Dean had to walk
along the altar, shaking the thurible and sending the incense
smoke everywhere. And when he'd that done, he had to do
the same thing, walking round the Bishop. But it wasn't the
delay that made us uneasy. It was the Dean himself. There
seemed to be a tension about his neck and a tightness about
his mouth as he swung the thurible, carried the book, moved
the chalices about. Once or twice when the altar boys were
slightly slow with carrying cruets or ringing the bell, he fired
them a glance that would have sliced meat. He reminded me
of a lion I'd seen in Duffy's Circus once that sat on a tub
staring at the trainer because he wouldn't let him out of the
cage to eat the audience. So the mass muttered on, the Dean
doing the hard bits, the Bishop taking over with his little

nose-in-the-air voice at the important bits. Finally it was time for the last gospel, and he wished us all a happy Saint Patrick's Day and gave us yet another blessing, only slow motion this time, and with words. To the organ making everything shake with 'Faith of Our Fathers', the Bishop was led in procession to the priests' refectory, to get out of his hat and finery and stuck into a heavy meal. The Dean, on his way out, made a discreet signal with his right hand to indicate we were to stay put. Three minutes later he came back.

We watched as he mounted the altar steps again, then turned to us. Not a cough or sniff was to be heard. When we felt we could hold our breath no longer, he spoke.

Whoever had booed, he said, was a blackguard. Only not just a blackguard. He was also . . . a blasphemer! He pinched his Adam's apple, leaving two dots that were first white and then red. Because the Bishop was a direct descendant of the apostles who were bishops also. So any boy who booed had in fact been booing the twelve apostles *and* our national saint, Saint Patrick, who had also been a bishop. What discourtesy! What heresy! He flicked back the cape of his soutane so the shiny bit showed. His lips were so tight you could hardly see them. A boy or boys like that were a disgrace to their school, their religion, their country, he said.

You could see boys staring, scratching their faces as he spoke. Right, then. The Bishop was descended from the apostles. OK. And the apostles were bishops . . . Or was it the bishops were apostles? Worse than the old riddle: Brothers and sisters have I none, but that man's father is my father's son. Only there was no time to think. The Dean was talking again.

He would, he said slowly, leave the chapel now. In fifteen minutes' time he would come back. If by then the culprits hadn't owned up, not one boy, not one single mother's son of a boy would set foot beyond the school gates this day. For all leave – he glanced from side to side, his voice almost a whisper – all leave to spend the day out in town would be cancelled. WAS THAT CLEAR? He glared at us for a full minute. Nobody coughed, nobody breathed. Then, with his eyes like burnt raisins in a rice pudding, he strode from the chapel.

When his steps had faded, a buzz filled the chapel. Cancel all leave! It wouldn't, it couldn't be allowed to happen. In my pew and the ones near it we all agreed: the Dean had gone mad. Not half-mad but whole-mad. For a start the Bishop and Saint Patrick were two entirely different men, anybody could see that. Did Saint Patrick ride around in a motorcar, for God's sake? The apostles had nothing to do with anything. Besides, it had been just a bit of booing. To listen to the Dean you'd think we'd been firing stones at the bloody Bentley.

After a couple of minutes of people twisting round in seats and pointing their fingers at each other's chests, the head prefect walked to the front of the altar rails. There he turned to face us with a raised hand like a traffic policeman, until the hum died down. This was, he said quietly, a simple matter. No call for anybody to go making it complicated. It was a simple matter of truth and lies. So to solve it the lies must be taken out and the truth told. In other words, let the culprits put their hands up now, make a clean breast and take their medicine. If they did, we'd know they were men and that honour wasn't just a word. If they didn't, we'd know they were cowards and honour was dead in this school.

Immediately a sixth-former with bad skin stood up and told the head prefect that his arse was dead. Hadn't everybody booed? What was the point in the head prefect going nya, nya, culprits this and culprits that, when *everybody* had booed? Shoulders hunched and hands open, he appealed to us. Half the congregation took the opportunity to nod in agreement with him. The other half sucked in their breath and began to tell anyone who would listen that *they* hadn't been doing any booing, and anyone who tried to say they did had – Just. Better. Watch it.

A fourth-year boy with red hair asked were we sure there'd *been* any booing? He'd been standing in the line like everybody else and *he* hadn't heard any. Cheering and clapping – he'd heard that. But not booing. For if there'd been booing, how come the Bishop hadn't said anything? Maybe it was all in the Dean's head. Maybe the Dean had a booing complex. After all, Joan of Arc had heard voices.

For a few seconds people weighed up this new possibility: brazen the whole thing out. Sure, wasn't the Dean a confusable man? Hadn't he been known on several occasions to start in on the rosary when he should have been saying grace before meals? If everybody else – every single person – was firm that no booing had happened, wouldn't the Dean's memory of what had occurred collapse? A small collective sigh indicated that the answer was no. Not even the Dean would swallow that notion – the booing was lodged too deep in his mind by now. And anyway, it wouldn't be ten minutes until at least twenty ginks had cracked and admitted to doing it. The red-haired fourth year who had made the suggestion was told to shut his face and not be stupid.

The head prefect held up his thin white hands. All right, he said. In that case blame must attach to whoever had *started* the booing. *They* must own up.

I twisted round in my pew. All the way back to the holy water font boys were glaring at each other. People were leaning forward, eyes staring, jaws thrust forward. Some were making chopping motions with their hands, and anger and suspicion were swelling by the second. Would the shifty eyes, the blushes, the shuffling of the culprit give him away? Hardly. This wasn't Greyfriars and besides, Billy Bunter only got six of the best from Mr Carruthers. Our Dean wouldn't stop until he'd torn the flesh from the bones of the guilty party.

Things had reached near-panic point when Vince McCullough rose from his place and strolled to the front. McCullough was a fifth year like myself, as skinny as a knitting needle, with watery-blue eyes and a slow grin. He was at once the luckiest and unluckiest boy in the place. If he broke a rule – listened to a crystal set, had a smoke behind the handball alley – the Dean always seemed to catch him. It got to the point where people stayed away from Vince because, with him, something bad happened. At the same time, he won things. He would make you any bet imaginable – like which side of the head Abraham Lincoln had been shot in, or which of two first years could pee the highest – and win every time. Now in the chapel McCullough gave the head prefect a mock salute, beamed at us and said he would take the blame for the booing.

A buzz several notches higher and sharper than the first one raced round.

'So was it you?' somebody called.

McCullough's grin, a slit in a turnip, broadened. Maybe he had booed, maybe he hadn't. Maybe *they* had booed. The point was, he was prepared to own up so everybody could be walking out the front gates – he looked at his watch – inside the next ten minutes. All he asked from us in return was a shilling each.

Another silence, then a fierce, surging debate, full of speeded-up gestures and hissing. The head prefect, his lips shiny with spittle, declared he was totally set against accepting any such offer, any such 'extortion bid', on moral grounds, and sat down in a dignified way. The rest of us sighed. Inside a minute and a half each pew of boys was passing money towards the centre of the chapel. The boy at the end of each row took their collection in cupped hands to McCullough, alone in front of the communion rails. Serious now, he transferred the money to a big brown paper bag he produced from his blazer pocket. Fifteen minutes later, raincoats over our arms and shamrocks lodged in our lapels, we streamed out the front gate. Back in school, McCullough was being led by the Dean to his room.

The breeze dropped as we moved down Bishop Street and the sun struggled out. At Wee Johnny's, where you could buy a single cigarette for a penny, we paused, lit up, felt the Brylcreem on our scalps begin to mix with a light film of sweat, sniffed the midday air. Along the city wall, at the base of Governor Walker's statue, a cluster of seniors had already gathered. Tobacco smoke was sucked in and sent whipping away. Heads swam. You could almost touch the freedom.

'His conscience was eating him,' a Woodbine from Aughnacloy said. 'That's why he stuck the hand up.' He spat and scraped his boot over the result.

'Booing a bishop's a reserved sin,' a Gallaher's Blue from Bellaghy pointed out. 'Ordinary priest can do damn all for you. Take another bishop to fix you up.'

The Fintona Senior Service's voice, when it spoke, was irritable. 'Reserved shite. Is booing bishops in the Ten Commandments? Or *Hart's Christian Doctrine*?' He raised a finger to stifle an objection. 'And *anyway*. McCullough never said he *done* it. All McCullough said was, he'd take the blame. Innocent until *proved* guilty.'

Brooding on this, we watched two girls pass, arms linked. They nudged each other and giggled, but no one had the heart to shout anything. Our minds were full of McCullough. McCullough grinning and receiving money, McCullough being led away, McCullough being murdered by the Dean. The thought throbbed like a boil.

In Fiorentini's the air was heavy with steam and hiss. We ordered chips, salt, vinegar, orange juice, to help us forget.

'Twenty-five quid he got,' someone said, trying to whistle through a mouthful of chips. 'Be able to afford a taxi to the hospital.' His snigger didn't catch.

We sat in our booths staring and silent, the bubble of cooking chips mixing with the jiggety-thud of 'Peggy Sue' on the juke box.

Afterwards, in the smoke and darkness of the pictures, it was a bit better. We watched carefully as Joan Collins, playing a shipwrecked nun, climbed onto a raft, wearing only a white nightshirt that showed her legs. Not a bit like the nuns we knew. Later there was a fight with a shark, where a Negro got dragged under the water and eaten, and just before he vanished it showed his mouth open screaming for help and blood running down his nose. Very satisfying. And when at the short intermission we bought tubs of ice cream from the girl, she smiled and her fingers touched ours. Like Joan Collins, she was a smasher – soft hands, nice smile, powerful headlights.

But then the clock above the door to the toilets showed half past five and we had to make a run for it. Coats over our arms, we sprinted back, boots hammering on the pavement and bouncing their noise off the terraced houses. At five to six, dusk closing in, we came gasping through the school gates. Barely time to hurl our coats into our rooms and collapse into our desks in the study hall. Two hours stuffed with Jane Austen and Latin verbs before tea time. And thoughts of McCullough. I stared at the grain in the desk top, tracing my pencil through the initials I had gouged early in the year. McCullough's desk, three over from mine, was empty. Had he been taken to the infirmary? Expelled? What a mad eejit like McCullough did couldn't be laid at our doorstep. And yet . . . Was it really fitting that one man should die for the people, even when that man had volunteered?

That question is still being asked. Even now, years after the Bishop has gone to his grave, the boys involved have left and grown middle-aged, the Dean has had his nervous break-down and been laicised – that story lives on with different endings. Some say the Dean took down a special long strap that left no marks and beat McCullough unconscious. Others, that the Dean noticed McCullough's pocket bulging and took every penny. A few people claimed McCullough used an old pocket watch to hypnotise the Dean and ar-ranged for him to forget everything when he woke up. Not many people believe that last one.

But in the weeks and months after, nobody knew what to think for certain. McCullough himself never spoke about it. But for three days he was different. Everywhere he went – class, the refectory, even the showers – he wore a pair of gloves. And the smile was gone. We assumed the gloves were to cover up the state of his hands after being slapped, but we didn't know for sure. The unsmiling face, though, was worst – with the mouth a straight line, your eyes went up to the way the skin stretched over his cheeks, to his fixed unblink-ing stare. To tell you the truth, I felt so bad I could hardly look at him.

But then, the way things worked out, I didn't have to, really. Easter was early that year, a week after Saint Patrick's Day. And when we came back there was a measles epidemic. The minute you showed spots they sent you home. Boys were borrowing pillows, eating toothpaste, breathing on each other to get their temperatures up. I was among the first wave of those sent home, and when I got back two weeks later, McCullough was sick and gone. So it was the beginning of June before our paths crossed again. I came on him alone one evening in the corner of the handball alley, his hand cupped round a half-cigarette, sucking hard. I took the butt when he offered it to me.

'How many matches would you say's in that?' he asked, pulling a Swan box from his pocket.

'Fifty. Between thirty and fifty.'

'A bob says twenty-five or less.' There were twenty-three. A ghost of a grin showed, then faded. Three weeks later he left school.

And the whole incident would have stayed buried in the mud at the bottom of my mind, forgotten, if I hadn't been at an art exhibition in Dublin last week. The art teacher in our school had a second ticket and kept at me to go, so I went. The exhibition was held in an old tarted-up brewery, where some great Irishman had once hidden, and all the paintings had this northern theme. And introducing things was the head prefect, only now he's the head painter. I'd seen him on the TV, being folksy but soulful. In the flesh he looked greyer and fatter. He told us all about the personal pleasure it had given him getting these marvellous Irish works together, living history, canvases that breathed invention. The audience clapped him until their hands were sore, especially the women.

Afterwards I was standing beside a watercolour cow with six legs, price £750, when I felt the touch on my shoulder. Same hands but whiter, with the bones bulging at the knuckles. If I'd been a millionaire he couldn't have been more excited. Good to see me, great occasion, how long was it? Ah, those days...Did I remember old so-and-so's Latin classes, and what about the porridge hahaaaaaa, and the cowboy films in the big hall, how the stagecoach wheels used go backwards, hahaaaaa? Dammit, I thought. I'll ask.

'Have you ever come across Vince McCullough? Had this big grin and was always betting,' I said.

His smile faded and he looked at the floor, shaking his head. 'Dead, I'm afraid. What, oh, eighteen months ago now. Met a lorry head-on near Cork. He was in the back seat – some woman driving. No seat belt on and . . . ' He spread his hands, helpless gesture. 'Windscreen.' There was a pause. 'Wife and him separated, of course.'

I tried not to think of McCullough's grin in a ditch somewhere. Buckled metal with smears of blood.

The head painter's soft voice dropped to a murmur. 'Superintendent down there I know, told me a funny thing. Seems his pockets were full of notes when they got him.'

'McCullough's?'

'Tens, fifties, hundreds. Near ten thousand. There was talk' – he leaned closer – 'talk of laundered money, drugs . . . Even, you know. The lads.' He smiled from the face that was plumper now. 'A man on the make till the end, our McCullough.' His eye caught somebody over my shoulder and he stuck out his hand, cultured and pale. 'Next time you're down, Jim, right? Lunch or something.' He patted my arm and was gone.

In the car on the way home I tried explaining to the art teacher why I wanted to pull the guts of Ireland's greatest painter up his throat and feed them to our Doberman. His white hands making fame and money, McCullough's beaten in boyhood and killed in middle age.

The art teacher rubbed condensation from the windscreen. 'You make it sound like the bloody road to Calvary. He's a bloody good artist, even you are jealous.'

With my eyes closed I could feel the car's throbbing movement under me, hear its hum. Was there a plan for us all? Or just things happening, the bones of our lives thrown in the air and falling in random patterns? McCullough's head, his hair stiff with dried blood, filled the darkness behind my eyes. The bruise made his grin lopsided, but his features were free of resentment.

OTHER FICTION TITLES

from

THE BLACKSTAFF PRESS

CLOCKING NINETY ON THE ROAD TO CLOUGHJORDAN

AND OTHER STORIES

•

LEO CULLEN

'Both subtle and funny . . . Leo Cullen memorably paints the
1950s picture of Connaughton's worlds, both the inner world
and that of the tinker camps, farms and crusty farmers and the
realities that drive him, in the emotional sense, at 90 miles an
hour along the back roads of Tipperary.'

OWEN KELLY, *IRISH NEWS*

'While Lally is a marvellous creation, the sensibility behind the
stories is predominantly that of a child, alive to the smells and
above all the changing light of the countryside; and what gives
the book its shape is the skilful way in which we are brought
gradually closer to the young Connaughtons. At first they are
merely passengers on family outings; then Lally junior
begins to take centre stage . . . the final effect is
atmospheric and poignant.'

ANTHONY GARDNER, *DAILY TELEGRAPH*

'At the conclusion I tried to remember when I had read a book
remotely like this before. I failed and then I tried to remember
when I had read a book as funny. I couldn't find one . . . the
author has assured himself a lasting place in comic Irish
literature . . . it's an unputdownable book . . .'

JOHN B. KEANE, *SUNDAY INDEPENDENT*

198 x 129 mm; 240 pp; 0-85640-537-X; pb

£5.99

VOICES FROM A FAR COUNTRY

•

HUGH CARR

Conor O'Donnell's world – the world he will 'make' from the 'clink and chatter' of encircling adults – is that of a small boy being reared in a south Donegal kitchen bar in the 1940s. Yet by using a kaleidoscope of shifting impressions – of singing and drinking, of rambling arguments about the war, of the electrifying rows between Conor's mismatched parents – Hugh Carr reintroduces us to the emotional and imaginative life that children live, inside and beyond the world of mere facts.

Hauntingly beautiful in its use of language and its evocation of the far country of childhood, this is an exceptional – and boldly original – first novel.

'The "Far Country" of playwright Hugh Carr's brilliant first novel is in fact two terrains. The first is that distant land called childhood, in this instance the childhood of Conor O'Donnell growing up in a south Donegal kitchen bar in the 1940s. The second is Donegal itself . . . a county of often harsh extremities which has traditionally existed as almost another country to Ireland. Combining an unmistakable lyrical gift with a dramatist's ear, Carr movingly details a bitter-sweet coming of age in a by-gone era.'
ANTHONY GLAVIN, *SUNDAY TRIBUNE*

'a real writer, whose ear for speech and pacing of prose combine the traditonal feel of a local ballad with the passion and insight of an older world'
LUCILE REDMOND, *IRISH PRESS*

210 x 148 mm; 304 pp; 0-85640-545-0; pb

£7.99

BLUE CHARM

•

BEN BIRDSALL

'These days are almost always grey but it is the endings of them that has the country like it is. There is little to compare with the surprising flush of colour after an afternoon drenched through by the rain and the horizon blurring into low swirls of mist – but yet there is in contrast this last triumph as the sky loses its dullness and the change of day comes on while you might be out walking the roads, altering the route so as not to be back in the house before the best part. Then to wait for the tension rising in the air and feel the surge of colour – only for that there would be no magic in the world at all.'

When John Davey inherits a small farm in remote Connemara he finds himself the centre of attraction with the locals as he battles to transform the ramshackle buildings into an artists' retreat. But as he is drawn into the gossip, comedies and tragedies of his neighbours' lives, he becomes part of a world where 'thoughts have no pattern'. Soon he discovers that there's more fun in imbibing 'mountain tay', fishing for trout and watching the 'blue charm' of the evening light, and that 'here it is not difficult to pass whole days with little achievement'.

Charged with the resonances of a fading Gaelic way of life, Ben Birdsall's sure-footed first novel captures a society caught between a haunted past and an unsteady future.

198 x 129 mm; 216 pp; 0-85640-544-2; pb

£7.99

THE HURT WORLD

SHORT STORIES OF THE TROUBLES

•

EDITED BY MICHAEL PARKER

The terror and dislocation of the Northern Ireland Troubles have left a legacy of anger, bewilderment and hurt. But they have also stimulated writing of the highest order: powerful, searching and painfully candid.

This timely new anthology of short stories is both a commemoration of that suffering and a celebration of that achievement. In story after story the best writers – Catholic and Protestant, women and men, exiles and natives – explore the stifling pressures of identity and tradition and the brutal impact of violence.

Because 'history can never be safely distant', editor Michael Parker has selected some stories which pre-date 1968, including work by Frank O'Connor, Michael McLaverty, John Montague and Mary Beckett, to give a historical context to the brilliance of more contemporary stories by, among others, William Trevor, Anne Devlin, Linda Anderson, Bernard Mac Laverty and Maurice Leitch.

An invaluable – and moving – contribution to the literature of the Troubles.

'The upside of Ulster's agony has been a permanent thread of literary excellence, well-demonstrated here in Michael Parker's judiciously-spread selection which sets writers of great repute (William Trevor, Bernard Mac Laverty, Anne Devlin) alongside lesser-known lights. These 20 stories are a timely reminder of what a complex subject can do to stimulate powerful, searching, and painfully candid artistry.'

SCOTSMAN

210 x 148 mm; 376 pp; 0-85640-557-4; pb

£12.99

ORDERING BLACKSTAFF BOOKS

All Blackstaff Press books are available through bookshops. In the case of difficulty, however, orders can be made directly to Gill & Macmillan UK Distribution, Blackstaff's distributor. Indicate clearly the title and number of copies required and send order with your name and address to:

CASH SALES

Gill & Macmillan UK Distribution
13–14 Goldenbridge Industrial Estate
Inchicore
Dublin 8

Please enclose a remittance to the value of the cover price plus: £2.50 for the first book plus 50p per copy for each additional book ordered to cover postage and packing. Payment should be made in sterling by UK personal cheque, sterling draft or international money order, made payable to Gill & Macmillan UK Distribution; or by Access or Visa.

Please debit my Access* Visa* account
*Cross out which is inapplicable

My card number is (13 or 16 digits)

Signature

Expiry date

Name on card

Address

Applicable only in the UK and Republic of Ireland

Full catalogue available on request from
The Blackstaff Press Limited
3 Galway Park, Dundonald, Belfast BT16 0AN
Northern Ireland
Tel. 01232 487161; Fax 01232 489552